Old Enough to Know Better

Old Enough to Know Better

Mal Pope

y Lolfa

First impression: 2010

The publishers wish to acknowledge the support of Cyngor Llyfrau Cymru

Cover design: Y Lolfa
Cover photograph: Daniel Lane

ISBN: 978 1 84771 291 2

Published, printed and bound in Wales
by Y Lolfa Cyf., Talybont, Ceredigion SY24 5HE
website www.ylolfa.com
e-mail ylolfa@ylolfa.com
tel 01970 832 304
fax 832 782

Foreword

I have watched Mal over the years in his work – he's a genius. He's one of the most prolific musician singer-songwriters I have ever met in my life. I have waited an age for this book to be published. I know that you will enjoy the read, as I have, but the most incredible part of Mal Pope is Mal himself. I love his work and I love the man…

Chris Needs MBE

Introduction

The little boy stood with four of his classmates. All of the other children in the room turned to see who had been asked to stand and either pulled faces or smiled as they took great pleasure in the embarrassing ceremony taking place before their eyes.

Prowling the room was the headmistress, Miss Jeffries. She was in her sixties, with beehive hair piled on top of her head like a portion of grey candyfloss, looking for all the world as if she had just walked from between the covers of *Jane Eyre*.

"These children…" she paused to stare at each of them individually. "These children… when it comes to reading…" She scanned them one last time. "…All of them have red warning lights over their head." The boy could feel his face start to glow, matching the colour of the apparent light above him. He wasn't sure if this was because he was being stared at by everyone in the room, or whether it was because, barely four miles away, his father sat, as head of the town's remedial school, and was charged with the responsibility of making sure the children of Swansea could both read and write. How on earth was he going to explain this?

Deliberately, she went on. "If things don't improve… they will not be allowed to take part in other school activities… like swimming lessons…" The young boy wasn't a big fan of water as the muddy marks on his legs and the back of his neck could prove. "Like chess club…" To be honest he quite liked draughts but chess seemed to be more hard work than fun. "Like football!"

"NO!"

To be honest he wasn't sure if he had shouted 'No' out loud or whether the thought was so strong in his head that he had only imagined it. Now was definitely not the time for defiance, Miss Jeffries wouldn't stand for that. Taking a deep breath he tried to gather himself and struggled hard to contain his urge to scream that banning football was too big a punishment for any child to bear.

Now, looking back over 40 years later, it does seem rather ironic that it was the boy's love for football and a desire to read the match reports from the sports pages of the *South Wales Evening Post* that finally turned Miss Jeffries' red light to amber, even if it never really got to be a shining green example of a literary genius.

That boy was me. Miss Jeffries probably thought I would never ever read a whole book let alone have the audacity to try to write one – but life can be strange. This story starts in a small town on the edge of nowhere and will show how dreaming out loud can take a boy who struggled to read at all, to end up reading Land Economy at Cambridge University. In a career that's lasted 37 years those dreams have allowed him to perform before prime ministers, film stars and even page three models; to travel around the world and to sing and play in some of the finest venues in the world.

As I look back over those years and the people who I have met and worked with it can sometimes feel like another life. I've often said if you were to read my CV the only name you wouldn't recognise was mine. So I give you fair warning and I make no apology that the sound of names being dropped will echo from almost every page.

I have always thought that life was a story and the more twists and turns that story takes, the more fortunate the man has been. If that is true then I really have been a very lucky man!

Mal Pope
Mumbles

Chapter 1

'Welcome to my world'

Just a mining town, on the edge of nowhere
These people saw me grow and they know my name
But I've been touched by Grace; I've been bathed in sunlight...

These are the opening words to the first song I wrote for the musical *Amazing Grace* which was based on the events surrounding the great Welsh Revival of 1904. They were written to give some background to the life of the revivalist Evan Roberts but like so many of my songs on records or in my musicals, the words bear more than a passing resemblance to my own life. When I was born in Brynhyfryd, Swansea in 1960 – the grandson of a miner who worked the seams which would eventually, literally, undermine the foundations of the house in which I was born – I couldn't have been more 'on the edge of nowhere'.

Translated into English, Brynhyfryd means Mount Pleasant. In days long gone the whole of the Swansea Valley must have been green and beautiful, with the river Tawe winding its way down from the Brecon Beacons, its crystal clear water spilling out onto the golden sands of Swansea Bay. The area has always had the ability to attract visitors, the Celts, Romans, Vikings all found reasons to come and settle. Following in these 'sandal prints', hundreds of years later, men and women came, drawn to the Welsh 'Klondike'. In these once pleasant pastures they would dig for coal or smelt the metal which would turn the town into an industrial powerhouse with a worldwide reputation and in the process turn the green fields brown, grey and black.

How clean the waters of Swansea Bay must have been before the industrial revolution. The Romans used to collect oysters in Swansea Bay and send them to the far flung corners of the empire. It was also the Romans who sowed the seeds of the destruction of 'Mount Pleasant', as it was they who took the news of Swansea's hidden minerals to the ancient world; they mined the metal ores of the Swansea Valley and sent them on the same journey as the oysters and, with that, the secret was out. By Tudor times, Swansea was well known as a place for tin-plating and copper-smelting. With a ready supply of coal from the surrounding valleys, limestone in abundance in nearby Mumbles and a navigable river and thriving port with which to import the copper ore from all around the world, the lower Swansea Valley was the perfect place to build the smelting works which would turn the Valley into the copper producing capital of the world. On these natural resources were built 'Copperopolis' or the 'Copper Kingdom'.

Contemporary descriptions liken the valley in the 1800s to Dante's poem 'Inferno'; likewise, paintings show green, smoke-laden clouds hanging over the brightly-lit smelting works. By 1960 that was all gone; what was left were the abandoned smelting works and a valley, bereft of trees, poisoned by chemicals. The ground was barren and pot-marked and the water that flowed from the local streams was a strange reddish colour; the legacy of discarded copper ore still seeped from the hills. In fact, when I first saw the pictures taken by the Viking landing craft of the surface of Mars, I have to say I found them strikingly familiar. They reminded me of the waste ground where I played out so many of my fantasies when I was a kid, in those summer holidays that used to last forever.

And so it was on a sunny day, in May 1960, that I became the third son of Stan and Meudwen Pope. When I was born my eldest brother David was seven years of age. He already had a reputation for being studious, with a love for reading and joy in learning that has never changed. Gareth was almost three and because of the closeness in our ages, he would be my constant companion and playmate whilst growing up. In fact, it was only on my fifteenth wedding anniversary that my wife finally became the person that I had shared a bed with for the longest time! My dad would conscientiously record the great family events on his old Philips reel to reel tape recorder. On the day I was born he duly asked both brothers about their feelings. David was measured and mature in his response. Gareth just asked "Can I kiss her!"

The house where I was born was the home of my grandparents George and Myfanwy Griffiths. The Pope family home was barely a mile away, but my mother had moved back home as my arrival become imminent. My grandmother was there from the day of my birth and she continued to play a major part in my life for as long as she lived.

Myfanwy Hopkins had come from a relatively well-to-do family. Her father was a successful coal merchant, but his real passion was music. At the turn of the twentieth century, music was more than just a pastime in that corner of Wales. The chapels prided themselves on their musical abilities and they were incredibly ambitious with their amateur productions. In his spare time my great grandfather David John Hopkins would teach piano and conduct the choir of Shiloh Chapel in Landore, a chapel that overlooked the smelting works. At Easter or Christmas he'd choose a major oratorio for the chapel to perform, like Handel's *Messiah* or *Elijah*. David John would conduct, with the choir being supported by a full orchestra which contained both of his daughters in starring roles.

Myfanwy passed numerous music exams and it still makes me smile to think that this woman, who never moved more than half a mile away from where she was born, had more letters after her name than anyone else in our family, then, or since. Her sister Ceridwen was a marvellous violinist. One of my strongest childhood memories is of a carefully preserved sepia newspaper cutting with a picture of Ceridwen as a very young girl in her best Sunday dress. She had a head full of 'Shirley Temple curls' and nestling under her chin was a very small violin. The article went on to say she had passed a violin exam with the best marks in the whole of the United Kingdom. The strange thing was that I never saw the adult Ceridwen so much as hold a violin let alone play any of her competition winning pieces.

The year 1904 saw the great Welsh Revival when chapel authority was challenged by a remarkable grass roots movement led by a troubled ex-miner named Evan Roberts. After eighteen months Evan would leave Wales, never to really speak again in public. But the results of his revival would shake the pillars of official religion in Wales for many years to come.

I'm not sure when Myfanwy had her religious conversion experience but it was a changing faith that she shared with George Griffiths. George's family was large, however the early death of his mother led to him being brought up by his auntie. George was no coal merchant; he was a simple miner, but he had a heart that could be trusted and there is absolutely no doubt that that heart belonged to Myfanwy. He was also bright, and despite having to leave school at an early age to go underground due to family circumstances, he was determined to educate himself. There wasn't a lot of free time in those days, but what time he found he used for studying, reading and re-reading his Bible to extract every last valuable nugget from that rich seam, in the same way that he worked the coal underground. Over the years, in chapel circles, he gained quite a reputation for being a Bible scholar and as a child I remember seeing his well-thumbed Bible covered in the smallest, finest notes that he had written in pencil on his beloved pages over the years.

When they married they had to make the decision as to

whether to stay in the big chapel – where my grandmother would play the massive pipe organ and consequently also play a central role in the social life of the area – or whether they should follow their conscience and join a little Gospel Hall, where the only instrument was a pump harmonium. Conscience won out and consequently the Gospel Hall became the centre of their world, as it would become the centre of the world for the rest of my family too.

If it hadn't been for the Gospel Hall, my mum and dad would never have met. My father Richard Stanley Pope, or Stan as every one called him, was born in Briton Ferry. His father Richard Glyn was a bacon hand in Lipton's and he married a local girl Gladys May after making quite a first impression on her by falling off his bike and landing at her feet. A smart, ambitious man, given to wearing spats or gaiters, he soon found Lipton's no measure for that ambition and so he saved and borrowed enough money to buy a grocer's shop in Pontrhydyfen, a little village in the Afan Valley. His new business, Pandy Stores, flourished and soon the Lord came calling. It wasn't long before Richard Pope put his hand into his pocket to help buy the land and then build the first Gospel Hall in the village.

Stan was Richard Glyn and Gladys's middle son. He was bright at school becoming school captain, but the war put paid to many of his ambitions. Whilst Stan was away in the navy Gladys was taken ill and died. This left his father Richard Glyn with a business to run and a young son, Colin, to care for. Richard Glyn soon married again but it was not long before he too was taken ill and sadly passed away.

Returning to Wales after being demobbed, Stan harboured dreams of continuing his studies, and the preferential treatment being shown to men returning from the forces guaranteed him a place in one of the leading universities in the country. Stan's young brother Colin was still living at home in Pontrhydyfen with his step-mother Ada. The shop was proving to be too much for the new family to run on their own and it soon became apparent that the business would either have to be sold or someone would need to be found to come in to run it. Losing the shop would have meant losing the roof over Colin's head and so Stan's dreams of university life were traded in for days spent cutting cheese, measuring out tea and trying to balance the books.

My mother Meudwen was also good at school. After doing well in her exams she trained to be a teacher. The war meant a shortage of teaching staff in London, so she, together with friends Eluned and Joyce, set off for the East End where she taught for a number of years.

In the meantime, Stan was gaining quite a reputation as a preacher. Every Sunday his grocer's van would travel along precarious valley roads as he travelled to his latest preaching engagement in some tin-shack gospel mission in areas from Swansea to the Rhondda Valley. Many people in the Gospel Hall circles thought that Stan and Meudwen would make a good couple, but it was at a holiday conference where the young people of the Gospel Halls went away to stay in a boarding school for a week, to share Bible study and friendship, that the couple finally became friends. Stan had noticed the pretty teacher and one night asked the boys in the dormitory if anyone knew this Meudwen Griffiths. "I should do," said a young man named Jonathon in the bed next to Stan's, "She's my sister".

The relationship wasn't without its hiccups. Stan's decision to occasionally wear a fashionable trilby didn't go down well with the modest Meudwen and soon that had to be discarded to maintain the relationship. It wasn't until years later that they found out that Myfanwy and George had actually accompanied them on their first date to the Mumbles, albeit from a safe, unknown distance. Meudwen was their only daughter and Stan was a grocer from the 'wild' valleys and I suppose this shows they must have had some concerns about the fitness of this young man to become their new son-in-law. Having said that, Stan must have passed the test as the young couple were married at Manselton Gospel Hall in 1949 and have recently celebrated their diamond wedding anniversary.

Stan's career as a grocer was not to last very much longer and, after arrangements were made for Colin's future, Stan eventually managed to finish off his education, training to become a teacher. So with both of my parents being teachers, education was always going to be important to them, even if it wasn't always my top priority.

CHAPTER 2

'These are golden days'

MY MOTHER WENT BACK to teaching when I was quite young, so I spent a lot of my early life in the company of my grandparents George and Myfanwy. 'Mam' and 'Dat', as we called them were possibly the sweetest people I ever knew. Utilising the grandparents' privilege of borrowing and then returning without too much damage, they moulded my actions without having the full responsibility for disciplining me that my parents had. So, the time spent with them always left me feeling completely spoilt. In the early Sixties the Welsh language didn't have the same standing in Welsh society as it has today. It was the language many still used at home but was not regularly used in business or in the media. It was a language that Mam and Dat felt completely at home with and because of that, it became my first language too, my 'grand' mother tongue you might say. There are reports from some people that they still remember me shouting out my needs and desires from my high chair in Welsh, but thankfully there are no recordings to prove this one way or another!

Although this was the decade when men would walk on the moon, my grandparents' house still only had an outdoor toilet and one fire which, not only had to warm the house, but also warm the water for washing. I don't want this to appear to be a scene from *How Green Was My Valley*, but the laundry really was done using a big tin bath and a massive plunger with which my grandmother would wrestle the dirt free from the clothes. My children still laugh at me because I can still recite to them the exact menu for any day of the week from those childhood days: Sunday – roast, Tuesday –

fish, Wednesday – casserole steak! Life was one long blissful routine that, together with our church commitments, meant that I had the security in my early life that many dream about but which I took completely for granted.

When it came to entertainment they had a radio which we always tuned into *Listen With Mother* after dinner and a gramophone player with recordings of the *Salvation Army at Christmas*, *The Sound of Music* and *Burl Ives and the Korean Orphans Choir*. But what was special and what again I took for granted was the piano. Mam was the most normal Welsh grandmother you could possibly imagine. Baking Welsh cakes and cutting bread so thin, as Max Boyce would say, it only had one side. But when she sat at the piano, she became someone completely different. A master of her craft, completely at home with the music with a touch that showed years of dedication and practice. Bach, Chopin, Beethoven and Liszt had been her musical companions from her earliest days. Later, they had been replaced by the hymn-tunes of Moody and Sankey when she moved to the Gospel Hall, but when she sat to play she could soon take herself back to the recitals she had given when she was a girl.

With teachers for parents, summer holidays were all spent together. Poppit Sands caravan park in west Wales became our holiday of choice and when we came home, time was split between playing football in the local park and helping my dad in the allotment at the bottom of the garden.

This blissful routine changed when my beloved grandfather died suddenly in 1967. Arrangements were made to extend my grandmother's house so that we could all move in together and an architect friend of the family, Philip Davies, drew up the plans. I don't think his daughter Hilary came to the house at that stage but it wouldn't be long before she was a regular visitor, but much more of that later. We moved into the new house in 1968, with Gareth and me sharing a bedroom and the same bed! One of the great things about moving was the enormous lawn at the front of the house where we played football together any spare moment we had.

It was around this time that my big brother David went on a school trip to Spain returning with bullfighting posters, a sombrero and an acoustic guitar. Being David, the first thing he did was to buy a book which taught him the basics, but before long I borrowed both the book and the guitar. David was the first one in our house to have a stereo and it was through his record collection that I found my own musical heroes: Simon and Garfunkel, Cat Stevens and Donovan. All had one thing in common, great songs based around the guitar.

At the age of seven I was playing the guitar and learning the songs these new heroes had written and by the age of nine I had started to write my own songs too. I suppose that might make me sound like some kind of freak but I think I was fairly normal. Brynhyfryd Primary School had a great reputation for producing fine football teams and I soon found my way into the team but music was becoming more and more important and that found a way for expression in school as well.

A young guitar-playing teacher had decided to start a school band. Anyone who could sing or play was invited to join him at lunchtime or after school. After constant nagging, my parents bought me a second hand guitar of my own for £3 and when I duly turned up at band practice I was welcomed with open arms. Peter Williams used torn-off pieces of his cigarette packets for plectrums and couldn't have been cooler or more encouraging. At school assemblies and special events throughout the year, the school band would perform anything from 'The Streets of London' to the old folk song 'John Riley'. Occasionally I would sing one of my own songs and, as always, the school would cheer our performances to the rafters. It wasn't exactly Beatlemania but it felt like it to a nine-year-old.

It was also around this time that something happened that would have a profound effect on me and would go on to influence almost every decision I have made over the last forty years. After years living a life of sin and debauchery, I found God at the age of eight. It was hardly one of those conversion stories you read in the tabloids about drug dealers or gang members coming to the end of the road and turning to the Almighty in their hour of need. There I was, a schoolboy whose only real vices were not wanting to wash behind his ears and reading comic books at night under the bedclothes with a torch when he should have been asleep, but it was an event that in my life can only be described as a turning point.

It was a November night in 1968 and a local evangelist, David Tucker, was the guest speaker at the six o'clock gospel service. He'd asked my big brother David to give his 'testimony' and as David told his story of finding his own personal faith I realised that I was the odd one out in our family. I mentioned it to my mum when I got home and after kneeling down at the side of the same bed in which I had been born eight years earlier, there I was, being born again. My mum was there on both occasions but I'm assured she screamed far less the second time around.

You might well argue that being born into that family, at that time, I was effectively brainwashed. You might think that it would have been more unusual if I had decided not to make that commitment. You may also ask what on earth an eight-year-old could know that would make such an experience have any credibility, and to be honest, on all of these counts, I would have to say that you have probably have got a point. What I do know is that whatever happened that night, real or imaginary, it has affected my decision-making ever since and still does. As this story develops, it might very well make sense of some of the decisions that I have made, because without the knowledge of my childhood conversion, some of the roads I've travelled, I have to admit, do seem rather strange.

Also, I have to say that making that decision at such a tender age has had its costs. Often I have felt I have not only been carrying the burden of trying to live up to other people's expectations, but also the unrealistic expectations I have placed on myself and my faith. As a child I grew up in a close knit community, where everyone knew my parents and what they stood for in our small community. Not only were they both teachers, they were both well-respected members of the Gospel Hall. There was a weight on my young shoulders of never letting the side down. I often remember the phrase "his father is a preacher you know" being used as a weapon against me when I didn't act exactly the way people thought I should have. On those occasions, my mind would always go to the Dusty Springfield song 'Son of a Preacher Man' and I thought, well he seems to be having much more fun than me.

The other part of the burden was my own desire to try to live up to the Bible's hero stories which I knew inside out:

Only a boy called David, only a babbling brook,
Only a boy called David, five little stones he took.

That was the chorus we learnt in Sunday school which helped us to remember the story of the little shepherd boy David who was the only one brave enough to face the giant Goliath. I knew the story so well, David fought and killed Goliath and went on to become the king, and I assumed live happily ever. It was many years later I read the rest of David's story; how he arranged the death of one of his most loyal soldiers in an attempt to cover up the affair he'd had with the man's wife Bathsheba. Now that didn't feature in any of the Band of Hope flannel graph presentations! I'm not trying to be overcritical of what I was taught – I was only a child and the stories certainly gave good moral guidelines. No, it's just that not being told the whole story gave me unrealistic expectations of myself and others. Trying to be the holiest kid in Brynhyfryd was an admirable ambition but one that was always doomed to fail and with that failure came the disappointment and sadness of not being able to live up to the goals I set for myself.

As the years have passed I have become more comfortable with being just another frail creature of dust and not the spiritual superhero of my dreams. I hope that over the years I've been a little easier on myself and easier on others when it comes to living up to those ideals. Being human means sometimes standing – it also means often falling. But it's the time you take to get up off the floor and start again which maybe gives us some idea of the faith we carry inside us. Of course, when you're eight years old life does seem a whole lot simpler. All I knew was that, at last, I was really part of the family. Anyway, enough of all that. I was still an ambitious kid in a hurry and we must get on with the story.

I was sad to leave primary school and Mr Williams' school band, but moving up to junior comprehensive school marked another turning point. If stardom wasn't going to find me in Swansea I would have to go out there and find it myself. There have always been talent shows and when I was a kid the big one was *Opportunity Knocks*. Every Monday evening Hughie Green would introduce a number of new acts. The clapometer would measure the volume of applause in the studio to show who the favourites were on the night, but it was down to the TV audience to send in their votes on postcards to choose the winner. Winning acts would often receive a record contract in a week and be top of the charts before their winning run had come to an end. Even some local people did well – Mary Hopkin went from being a Pontardawe teenager to number one in no time at all but it was the winning run of Neil Reid, a twelve-year-old singer from Scotland that made me think it was time to think bigger. If he could be an *Opportunity Knocks* winner, then so could I.

I sent off an application to the TV show and was given an appointment for an audition in a Cardiff hotel. All I really remember about the whole affair was the guy before me wouldn't take no for an answer. He kept on taking pieces of music out of his bag and only just fell short of begging for the chance to appear on the show. Even as a twelve-year-old I was embarrassed for him. When they eventually got rid of him I realised the time had come for me to stand in front of the panel. I said I was going to sing a song that I had written myself and when I finished there was silence. The secretary ushered me out and said if successful I would receive a letter within fourteen days. Every day I checked the mail and after three weeks I realised, they didn't want me.

Opportunity Knocks wasn't the only audition I had. A letter offering me an audition came out of the blue from Eric Wetherell, the resident musical director for HTV, the independent TV station based in Cardiff. I was never quite sure how this came about but it might well have been through a family connection. One of my dad's boyhood friends from Pontrhydyfen had been the singer Ivor Emmanuel, probably best known for his role in the film *Zulu* where he started the singing of 'Men of Harlech'. He had been a big star at HTV presenting their Sunday evening network show *Land of Song*. I had written to him at some stage (without receiving a reply) telling him of my hopes to follow in his musical footsteps. I always thought that maybe he had had something to do with it.

I turned up at the Pontcanna studio for a late-night audition armed with my guitar. I walked into a TV studio for the first time in my life to be greeted very courteously by Mr Wetherell. There was an accompanist ready to take my music but when I told them I played the guitar and sang songs I had written myself, I'm sure they must have been horrified. They allowed me to play a couple of songs and then we spent some time talking about the type of music I liked. Mr Wetherell said he would give the audition some thought and some days later a second letter arrived. It was a very nice letter, but in essence he was suggesting I go for guitar lessons. He was probably right but I was determined to plough my own field and as I didn't really enjoy the piano lessons I had already been forced to take, starting guitar lessons really didn't interest me.

HTV
CYMRU WALES

HTV CYF Y GANOLFAN DELEDU CAERDYDD CF1 9XL TELEFFON 0222 26633 TELECS 9330 HAR CAERDYDD
HTV LIMITED TELEVISION CENTRE CARDIFF CF1 9XL TELEPHONE 0222 26633 TELEX 49330 HAR CARDIFF

April 19th, 1972.

Mr. Maldwyn Pope,
Grittleton,
10 Penfilia Terrace,
Brynhyfryd,
Swansea.

Dear Maldwyn,

Thank you for coming in to audition to us on April 17th.

I hope very much that you intend to study the guitar with a teacher. As I explained to you, a teacher can save you a great deal of time by pointing out from his own experience things which you would take much longer to find yourself.

I think you have a great deal of promise and I have heard of a good teacher in Swansea. I would be grateful if you would ask your parents to get in touch with me, as I think a matter such as this concerns them as well as you.

Yours sincerely,

Eric Wetherell

Eric Wetherell.
Music Director.

There we are then, my career as a pop star was over. I would just have to be content with a career as a professional footballer instead. The football was going well. I might not have been the most skilful player but I was determined and very fast, winning the town 100-yard sprint two years running whilst at primary school. My parents were always very supportive but, as they kept saying, football and music were all very well but no one was going to make a living doing either of those jobs! What I needed was a good education and good exam results. As you can imagine, with both parents being teachers, my lack of academic achievement and effort led to extra long silences as they read my end of term reports.

Chapter 3

'Do ye ken John Peel?'

There are certain events that happen to us which, although they might seem quite inconsequential at the time, can set the direction for the rest of our lives. From that moment on life will never be the same again. It might be an unexpected encounter, a phone call or a letter. For me it was a chance remark made in 1973 by a friend of my eldest brother David, a long-haired guitarist named Mike Nicholson.

That year was already turning into a great one for me. As I approached the start of my teenage years I have to say life was organised, very busy and extremely happy. The three most important things in my life were God, football and music, probably in that order. Our family life revolved around our church commitments. My grandmother Myfanwy still played the harmonium for every service; my dad was an elder at the Gospel Hall and also the Sunday school superintendent where he was assisted by my mum. We all had our 'reserved' seats and responsibilities which the three Pope boys took very seriously.

Sunday might have been designated as being a day of rest in the Good Book but for the 'Popes' it was probably the busiest day in the week. Our family routine meant I went to the little Phillip Street Gospel Hall in Manselton three times on a Sunday – the morning meeting was at 11 am, Sunday school at 3 pm and then the gospel service started at 6 pm. We had the prayer meeting on Monday at 7.30 pm, and on Wednesday evenings the six o'clock Band of Hope meeting was followed by Bible Study at 7.30 pm. No wonder that by the age of eleven I could recite all sixty-six names of the books of the Bible in order. Saturday was school football in the morning and junior league in the afternoon and the rest of the time I continued to practise the guitar and write songs.

Up to this point the greatest moment in my life had been my selection to captain the Swansea Schoolboys under-13 football team, a side that went unbeaten all year, eventually winning the Welsh under-13 championship. It was a team full of players that would go on to achieve great success in the professional game. Jeremy Charles, son of Welsh international Mel and nephew of the gentle giant John Charles, was one of my best friends and a superb all-round athlete. Russell Coughlan was one of the most naturally talented players I'd ever seen and he, together with another team member, Steve Lovell, also went on to carve out long term careers in the game.

Looking back now, I realise I must have seemed a very strange team-mate. I always refused to swear, no matter how much I was provoked on or off the pitch. As a family we preferred to give money to the club rather than buy their raffle tickets because raffle tickets were 'technically' gambling and I was always ready with my excuses for why I wasn't able to join them on a night, because... well I was at chapel wasn't I? I must have been the most devout midfield player in junior football.

Having said that, I did have a reputation for being not entirely 'meek and mild' when I passed the white lines on the side of the pitch. It was more 'wrath and justice' than 'mercy and forgiveness' when the 'Pope' played against you. I have to say I always strove to be 'firm but fair' – if the tackles were late, I assure you that I got there as fast as I could and I'm pretty sure anyone I tangled with back then would have to say I always tackled with a smile on my face! Looking back, with the 20/20 vision hindsight gives you, I can actually pinpoint the moment my footballing career peaked. It was an October afternoon in 1972. I was captaining the Swansea Schoolboys side at the Vetch Field, home to Swansea City. I'd played there a number of times in the past, picking up a ten shilling note on two occasions when my parents rewarded me for scoring on the hallowed turf. The reason I'm so sure this was the moment I peaked was that my dad was standing on the side of the pitch when Roy Bentley, the legendary captain of the 1950s Chelsea league championship winning side came to stand next to him. As Swansea manager he was casting his eye over the potential schoolboy talent. "Who's that kid making all the tackles in midfield?" he asked my dad. "Maldwyn Pope," he said proudly without saying he was my dad. Mr Bentley took out a notepad and scribbled down the name. Within a week he'd been sacked by the Swans and I'm sure that with Roy went my chances of becoming a professional player.

Being the youngest of three brothers meant that I was always the last who was old enough to do the grown up things. And, as if I didn't go to church enough already, there were two meetings where I was not welcome. These were the youth gatherings on a Friday and Sunday evenings where all of the church kids got together in Treboeth Gospel Hall on the north side of Swansea, the most modern and well-furnished hall in the area. 1973 meant I was finally allowed to join in and I loved it.

One of the main reasons I looked forward to the meetings was that afterwards we were all invited back to Mike Nicholson's house for squash, biscuits and the occasional hot dog. Mike's parents had an 'open house' for the youth and on Fridays and Sundays there were a constant stream of kids turning up and making themselves at home. 'Mike Nick', as everyone called him was the coolest Christian I had ever met. He had really long hair, past his collar and he played the guitar better than anyone I've ever heard. During those evening get-togethers Mike would get his guitar out and people would take it in turns to play a song.

I suppose at twelve I didn't realise that there was probably some sort of etiquette involved so when I was handed the guitar, I didn't pass it on. The wounds of the disappointment at failing to make it onto *Opportunity Knocks* and the gentle rejection from HTV had healed and I just thought to myself, I've got some songs that I've written that I'd like to play. Since I'd been writing songs for three years I had quite a selection to choose from. As the weeks went past, the more I became a regular turn at Mike Nick's house and the encouragement shown to me by Mike, my brothers and the other kids led to more songs being written to show off new material to the group.

It was a few weeks later that Mike Nick came up with the suggestion that would change my life forever. "You ought to send a tape of these songs to John Peel, he'd love them." Now to be honest I didn't know who John Peel was. I listened to Radio 1 from dawn to dusk and counted Tony Blackburn, Johnnie Walker and 'Diddy' David Hamilton as some of my dearest friends but John Peel's *Sounds of the Seventies* show didn't start until 10pm and at twelve years old that was way past my bedtime. I remember going to my big brother David and asking what Mike Nick had meant. He explained that John Peel was, in the opinion of every sixth-former in Britain, the coolest DJ on the air. He had a late-night radio show; he only played alternative music, none of that commercial teeny bop stuff and was based at the BBC in London. It all seemed very simple, I would make a tape and send it to him and he would make me a star.

Without telling my parents I borrowed my dad's prized Philips tape recorder and recorded a selection of the songs that seemed to receive the best reaction from the kids on Friday and Sunday evenings. I sent it off with a brief letter outlining my age and the fact that I had written all of the songs from personal experience.

It was a Saturday morning in May when the letter arrived. It was in a BBC envelope and my mum brought it straight up to me in bed. I could feel the electricity flowing through my hands as I opened the letter. By the age of thirteen I had already experienced the rejection that inevitably follows every musician but I still dreamed that one day my break would come. The letter read as follows:

BBC

BRITISH BROADCASTING CORPORATION

BROADCASTING HOUSE LONDON W1A 1AA

TELEPHONE 01-580 4468 CABLES: BROADCASTS LONDONPS4

TELEGRAMS: BROADCASTS LONDON TELEX TELEX: 22182

23rd May 1973

Master Maldwyn Pope,
Grittleton,
10 Penfillia Terrace,
Drynwyfryd,
SWANSEA SAS 9HJ

Mr. John Walters,
318 Egton House,
Langham Place,
London,
W1A 1AA

Dear Maldwyn,

John Peel has gone away for a few days but both he and I were able to hear your tape and were impressed with your work. We would like you to record some songs for us with a view to broadcasting them on John Peel's "Top Gear" programme.

Could you ask your father to write to me giving his permission for you to appear and if possible a telephone number, so that we could arrange a date when you might come to London and record.

Yours sincerely,

JOHN WALTERS,
Producer - "Top Gear"

It was only some years later that the broadcaster Paul Gambaccini, a close friend of John Peel, told me the full story and why it had taken them a number of weeks to reply. John Peel received countless demos every day of the week. Most were from English postgraduate students or aspiring 'prog' rock bands. When my letter and tape arrived at the BBC, John Peel and his producer John Walters were so intrigued by the idea of a twelve-year-old singer-songwriter that they couldn't wait to play the tape expecting the very worst. The trouble was that my dad's prized tape recorder was so old that Radio1 didn't have a machine capable of playing it. Eventually, one was found in a forgotten basement in Broadcasting House and when they did eventually hear it, they were apparently captivated by the strange Welsh boy soprano singing his own love songs. The reason John Peel had gone away for a few days was that on 23rd May 1973 his beloved Liverpool won the UEFA Cup and I assume he had gone to see them play Borussia Mönchengladbach.

Being a Saturday I had to wait a whole two days for Monday to come round and for my dad to make the call. When he came off the phone the deal was done. I would have a day off school and go to record at the BBC in London. I would not go alone. This was going to be an outing for all three boys, David, Gareth and Maldwyn. We would all be bought new trendy outfits and would travel British Rail second class at the BBC's expense (in fact they would only pay for two tickets, so my mum and dad paid for the extra one). They were of a mind that this was a one-off experience of a lifetime and that all of the Pope boys should enjoy it together.

CHAPTER 3

'Didn't we have a lovely time the day we went to London?'

By this time my brother David was studying Mathematics at Cambridge University and at nineteen, in my eyes, he was a grown up. He could drive, had a girlfriend and the fact that he occasionally wore a deerstalker just made him all the more impressive. He acted as our tour manager, got us from Paddington station to Broadcasting House safely and bought us all burger and chips at Wimpy.

I still remember waiting for John Peel's producer to come to collect us from reception. Walters was a big-bear of a man, warm and funny and I suspect quite intimidating if you were a 'grown up'. But to me he was just like the ringmaster at the circus, loud, brash and full of show business. He ushered us in to meet John Peel who wore a light-blue denim pair of dungarees which had a Liverpool badge sown onto the chest and hair that was even longer than Mike Nick's. Whereas Walters was loud and demonstrative, John Peel was quite the opposite, quiet, even shy. By this stage I had actually heard the programme that I was going to record a session for, but I still didn't quite understand why the loud guy was the producer and the quiet man was the star.

The first part of the afternoon was going to be a guided tour of the Radio 1 studios. I was pretty devastated that Tony Blackburn had already left for the day but delighted to be introduced to Jimmy Young as he left the building to catch a cab home. I had travelled to London armed with a guitar and an autograph book, both of which I still have and, after shaking Jimmy's hand, I thrust the book at him. The pen I had brought was about to run out of ink, but he managed to scrape his name onto a clean page and made my day. Whatever else happened, at least I had Jimmy Young's autograph to show the kids in school.

Johnny Walker was presenting his lunchtime programme and we spent a few minutes watching how the whole thing worked. Turntables, banks of jingle cartridges – it was like taking a trip into mission control as far as I was concerned. For the past couple of years I had been listening to these guys every day and now, here I was, right at the heart of things seeing how the magic was made.

After the meet and greet came the session. The studio was 'Langham 1' and it had been booked for the whole of the afternoon. I couldn't believe it, all that time to record six songs. The first thing that happened was that I had to pose at the piano next to John Peel. He decided to take hold of some of my lyrics as if reading them and the picture shows John, somewhat uncharacteristically, smiling at the camera.

I had been playing the songs for some time at various events at church and school and knew them inside out. To be honest I can't recall any feelings of nerves or being anxious. Within an hour or so we were finished and ready to head back to Paddington. The two Johns were aware that, as a minor, I wouldn't receive a full session fee for the recordings. I always thought, typical, I come from Wales and they want to treat me as a minor! We all traipsed back to their office which was covered from floor to ceiling in records to see if they could give me some 'booty' to make up the shortfall. John Peel spent a good fifteen minutes rooting around for as much interesting stuff as he could find, from singer-songwriters Jim Croce and Neil Diamond, to the sitar playing of Ravi Shankar and the progressive rock of Barclay James Harvest. They divided out the haul between the three brothers and then we left for Wales.

The train journey back to London passed in a blur. We talked over and over about how strange the experience had been and about all the people we had met. Dad met us at the station and then we went over the whole day again for my parents before going to bed – well, I did have school in the morning.

The next few weeks were a strange time. The session had been scheduled for Tuesday 10th July 1973. Everybody in school knew that I'd been to the BBC in London. Lots of them thought I'd made a record already. Some thought I was going to be on *Top of the Pops*. It must have been a difficult time for my parents and the culture they came from. They wanted to support me as much as possible but looking back now I realise they must have come in for a lot of criticism from various sections of the church community. In fact, I later found out that some Gospel Halls never asked my dad to speak at their services again. They frowned on cinemas and television, and for one of their own to be featured on a radio broadcast singing pop music was quite frankly shocking. One of the parents in the school wanted to contact the local paper to ask them to write an article about the upcoming broadcast. My parents politely, but firmly refused. This was going to be a one-off. Although they were very proud of my achievement, there wasn't any need to tell the whole world.

I tuned into Radio 1 early on the morning of 10th July and throughout the day the advertising trailer for *Sounds of the Seventies* came on mentioning my name. I must have been pretty exhausted by the time of the broadcast, but we all sat around the radio as a family and turned on our little cassette machine to record the songs as they came on. For any one looking on, it must have looked like a scene out of *The Waltons*.

There were six songs in the session and they were interspersed between John Peel's regular fare of avant-garde artists such as Gerry Rafferty, Thin Lizzy and Roxy Music!

What my grandmother must have been thinking I can only imagine. John Peel was incredibly generous. He said that he had rung all of his friends to listen to the session and that my age didn't matter, it was the songs that counted. I went to bed that night thinking that this was it. I'd seen *Opportunity Knocks*. Within a week I'd be a recording artist and by the end of the month I'd be No. 1.

What I have subsequently learnt is that it's the waiting that's the hardest part. I returned to school the next day and some people had heard the session, but most hadn't because it was so late. Everyone wanted to know what I was going to do next. The answer was nothing. No one was ringing offering a record deal, in fact with the school holidays looming I was starting to think that Jimmy Young's autograph might just be it, after all.

CHAPTER 4

'Rocket Man'

IT WAS SOME WEEKS later that the wheels started to turn again. John Walters rang to say that there had been some interest shown in the session by a number of record labels. The two most interested record labels were both relatively new. The first had released and secured their first hit with an instrumental album called *Tubular Bells*. Virgin Records was new and the people running it, including Richard Branson, were also fairly new to the industry. In John Walters' opinion the equally newly-formed Rocket Records company would be a better bet. Rocket Records had been founded by the team surrounding Elton John as a vehicle to release albums by people who were associated with Elton but didn't have deals at the time.

The company was being run by Steve Brown who had first spotted Elton John's potential when he worked as a publisher at DJM Records. In fact when Elton played his first songs to Steve, he said they were awful and that Elton should go away and write some more. Instead of running away to lick his wounds Elton, together with co-writer lyricist Bernie Taupin, wrote a whole new batch of songs which Steve loved so much so that he produced Elton's first album *Empty Sky*. From that moment on Steve had been a close confidant of Elton's and was the obvious choice to run the newly-formed record company.

John Walters was also very aware of my family background and my parents' concerns and the clinching factor for everybody was that Steve Brown had been brought up as a member of the Salvation Army (his father had actually been a Major in the movement). In fact, in those early days when Elton was a struggling singer-songwriter, he quite often stayed at the Salvation Army hostel in Oxford Street run by Steve's dad, instead of making his way home to Pinner. In a world of sex, drugs and rock and roll, this really did seem like a marriage made in heaven.

By this stage we were into the school summer holidays and, taking a break from Poppit Sands, my parents together with Gareth and me, headed for the north Wales seaside resort of Llanfairfechan. My dad had been asked to phone Steve Brown during the week and I still remember him coming out of a telephone box smiling and looking apprehensive at the same time. Steve Brown had been charming on the phone. He understood all of the concerns my parents had, but told him that everyone at the record company loved the songs and they wanted to record an album with me. Arrangements were made for Steve to travel to Swansea the following week together with John Walters to record every song I had written.

Herein lay the first problem, Steve wanted us to book a recording studio in Swansea. As far as we knew there wasn't one in Swansea in 1973. In the end, Steve brought down a Revox tape recorder and some mikes and my dad let us use one of his school classrooms which were empty during the school holidays. Steve wore a white suit, had collar length hair and a Mexican moustache. He was just so glamorous and he talked about Elton and America and it all sounded fantastic. As well as bringing a tape recorder, he also brought a selection of Elton's albums and over the coming months I would learn every song, word for word and note for note.

My grandmother had laid on a typical Welsh spread for our guests from London: ham, beef and chicken, all sliced in her inimitable way, only to find out that Steve was a vegetarian. I mean we'd read about them but never met a real one! Before they left Steve produced the contracts for recording and publishing. They would both be five-year deals and John Walters assured us that they were absolutely fair. In fact Rocket prided themselves on offering the artists a far greater royalty than any of the other record companies did at that time. We signed on the dotted line and that was it – I was a thirteen-year-old from Swansea with a worldwide recording contract. My dad and I took Steve and John back to the station and waited, and waited.

Rocket Records was an incredible idea born in a time of idealism and innocence and was set up to work on a completely different model to the record companies that had existed up to that point. Elton John had found success as a recording artist for DJM Records. DJM had been founded by Dick James who, before moving into the business side of music, was most famous for singing the theme song to the TV series *Robin Hood*. Dick had really made his fortune as a publisher when he set up Northern Songs to publish the work of the Beatles and he used that fortune and influence to help establish Elton as a successful solo artist. But Dick was from a different era and had a different business mentality. The artist worked for the publisher and record company who, quite often, received the lion's share of the rewards. As artists grew in confidence and maturity, this became an increasingly difficult model to sustain. The result was that Dick James fell out with the Beatles and eventually Elton John as well, as the artists looked for more control and a greater share of the money their work generated. Dick James never really understood why his writers and artists would become so ungrateful after all he had done for them. The world had moved on and music business moguls such as Dick James found themselves bypassed and rejected by those they felt they had created.

So the early 1970s was the ideal time for a new record company model, run by people who loved music, and wanted the best for their artists. They had already signed a number of acts including Kiki Dee, a band called Longdancer (featuring a very young Dave Stewart who would go on to find fame with the Eurythmics) and Davey Johnstone, who was the guitarist in Elton's band. To add to that distinguished stable, a thirteen-year-old schoolboy from Wales must have seemed quite a risk, but this was the early 1970s and I think I might have appeared to be quite a cool addition at the time. As the news spread to the music papers, Elton was interviewed by the music press about his new protégé. He was quoted as saying that he had been contacted by John Peel and told about the strange young Welsh singer-songwriter. At this stage Elton was having a bit of a problem with the name Maldwyn Pope, so he called me 'Boldwyn Pig' instead. He said that after hearing the session on Radio 1, they had decided to do a 'Hughie Green', as a reference to the TV show *Opportunity Knocks* and rush down to darkest Wales to sign me up!

That might have been the way it seemed to Elton, but to me, each week that passed seemed like an eternity. Eventually, on 29th September, a letter arrived with the arrangements made for my first recording session. As well as the letter there was also a cheque for £200. This was my advance for signing the new deals. It wasn't the million pound deals you often hear bandied around these days, but back in 1973 that seemed like an awful lot of money to a teenager. My dad opened a bank account in my name and the bank manager responsible for opening the account in Swansea said that he had also been responsible for opening a bank account for one John Lennon, when he used to work in Liverpool. What a good omen we all thought. Convinced that this was the first cheque of many, we put it safely in the bank where it stayed for many years, steadily losing its value as inflation gripped the economy. It was decided that I would go to London during the autumn half term holidays in early October and having to wait for a whole half term of school to pass only made the time drag even more.

CHAPTER 5

'We're gonna make you a star'

I'M NOT SURE EXACTLY what I expected to happen on my first week in London as a Rocket Record artist, but what I do remember is it surpassed every dream. My big brother David was to act as chaperone for the week and when we got off the train in Paddington, we were met by everyone from the record company. It was like one big party, very similar to the feeling I used to get on the annual Sunday school outing. The only difference was that instead of a south Wales double-decker bus, we would travel around London in a white Rolls Royce. Steve Brown was there as master of ceremonies and he was joined by secretaries and record company staff who all wanted to make us feel welcome.

Our chauffeur was a young record plugger at Rocket by the name of Clive Banks. Clive would later go on to be managing director of Island records and manage Simple Minds and even at this early stage in his career, you could tell by the way he dressed that he was a man on his way to the top. Elton was on tour in America at the time and Clive was a good friend of Dee Murray, the bass player in the band. Dee had left Clive in charge of his Roller and everyone thought it was a good idea to impress their latest signing by using that instead of a black cab. We all travelled back to Wardour Street in convoy and went straight to one of the most expensive French restaurants in Soho.

We had a long table for the whole of the company and I was given the place of honour next to Steve Brown the boss. I couldn't make head or tail of the menu. I was trying to find something that looked vaguely familiar because, as I was still in school, my level of French really was of the schoolboy variety. When you consider that up until that moment in my life, the only meal outside my family home had either been in the school canteen or maybe in a local café – the French menu really was all Greek to me. In the end Steve, probably against his vegetarian principles, ordered me something similar to steak and chips. The chips were a little thin compared with the ones my grandmother would make or those that we would get from the local fish and chip shop, and the steak was covered in some red sauce which I discreetly scraped off before tucking in. It was probably at this time that I realised that ice cream was a pretty safe bet at any restaurant and it's still something I order with confidence even now.

After lunch we went back to 101 Wardour Street, the home of Rocket Records. Even the record company logo was different to all of the major record companies at the time. The directors of Rocket had chosen a cartoon-like image of a small steam engine pulling coaches with the name Rocket Records Company. The engine had a *Thomas the Tank* engine-like smiley face, with a winking eye on the front. I remember that when Steve Brown showed it to me on his first visit to Swansea, I said I really liked it – if that didn't appear a childish thing to say. At thirteen, I don't think I completely saw the irony in my own statement.

The brightly coloured logo was painted on the mirrored doors at the bottom of the steps to the upstairs office. We walked into the offices and it was everything I imagined it would be. There were walls covered in gold discs, record decks made from gold spinning parts; they even had a gigantic wicker peacock chair which was reserved for Elton himself. On the back of one of the big leather chairs was a hand written notice saying 'Kiki Dee 514 sales'.

Elton had always been a big fan of Pauline Matthews from Bradford. In later years she told me that they had first met when they were both singing cover versions of the latest pop hits in the late Sixties on the budget albums that filled the shelves of Woolworths. All she could really remember about him was that he dressed a little strangely; that he wore glasses and that he was so shy that he didn't really say very much to her. Elton's future manager John Reid had been in charge of the UK arm of Motown Records when Pauline, or Kiki Dee as she was now known, became the first white artist to join that label. When he left he officially introduced her to Elton and they became good friends. Kiki's recordings for Motown hadn't been very successful, but Elton had fallen in love with her voice. When Rocket was created, Kiki was top of the list of people Elton wanted to support. He produced her first album *Loving and Free*, encouraged her to write her own material and, together with Bernie Taupin, even wrote a number of songs for her. The first single release was one of Elton's songs called 'Lonnie and Josie' which is still one of my favourite songs written by them and recorded by another artist. Again that had failed to chart and it fell to a rather strange song to actually give Kiki Dee her first hit record. One of the most haunting songs on the album was a translation of a French song called 'Amoureuse'. The fact that it had sold 514 copies the previous day meant that Rocket was on the way to having its first hit single. It seemed everything that Elton was touching was turning to gold.

I spent that afternoon in the company of the Rocket Records press officer Penny Valentine. For the next few years Penny was like a surrogate mum and big sister to me at Rocket and I think looking back, if I'm really honest, I probably had quite a bit of a crush on her as well – if that doesn't sound too weird. Penny really was the archetypal 1960s "IT" girl. It's been said that Penny was 'the first woman to write about music as if it really mattered'. Because of her looks and ability she quickly became a firm favourite with the up-and-coming bands of the Sixties. Apparently when the Beatles travelled to London to promote their early singles, one of the trips they looked forward to most was to the offices of *Disc* magazine where they would 'ogle and fawn' over the lovely Penny.

Penny spent the afternoon asking me lots of questions about my life and the music. I found the whole thing rather odd. Being the youngest of three boys, my parents were always interested in what I got up to, especially when it came to school, but here was an adult asking me quite searching questions and treating me like an adult for the first time in my life. All of this questioning was for Penny to write my biography which would later be sent to the press when my first recordings were released. This is what Penny wrote in October 1973 (right).

With the 'biography' completed, Steve Brown grabbed a camera and we left the office for my first photo shoot. As well as being a record company executive and record producer, Steve had also taken quite a few photographs of Elton in the early days – so I was in safe hands.

My brother David and I headed off to the Cumberland Hotel in Marble Arch where we were to stay for the whole of the week; the hotel would become my home every time I visited London. It certainly had been quite a day.

THE ROCKET RECORD COMPANY Ltd.

101 Wardour Street, London W1V 4QD Tel: 01-437 5047
01-437 7092

MALDWYN POPE

Discovered by John Peel, who featured him on 'Top Gear' earlier this year, Maldwyn Pope was born in Swansea on May 18th, 1960.

His Welsh upbringing - the hymns in chapel, the poetry and music so much an inherant part of Welsh life - have naturally had an enormous effect on him. And it's this influence that emerges most in both his music and lyrics.

Maldwyn Pope may only be 13 years old, but his music reflects the simple perceptions of his age and sets him well apart from his 'teenybop' contemporaries.

Maldwyn was born into a family where music was an everyday part of life, where a piano was a necessary part of the furnishings. His great-grandfather a famous composer of Welsh hymns, his grandmother and aunt proficient organists, it seemed only natural that Maldwyn would follow in the footsteps of his older brothers Gareth and David and learn piano.

He started lessons at 8. A year later he gave them up because, he says, they were too boring. That same year, at 9, Maldwyn was writing his first songs and playing an acoustic guitar brought back from Spain by David.

At his primary school - Brynhyfryd - he played in a band organised by his bongo-playing teacher. At Manselton Junior Comprehensive he began organising concerts. But still music was more of a sideline than a burning ambition.

Through all his schooling Maldwyn showed not only brilliant skill academically, but was quickly pin-pointed as a natural football talent. At junior school he was in the school team - setting up an all-time record by being in the fourth year team when he was only in the second year stream. He went on to play for the Swansea schoolboys Under-11's; became captain of the Under-13's; played for the Under-15 schoolboy squad. He seemed set for a solid career on the football field.

Now, he says, his ideas have changed. Writing his songs is now taking up more and more of his time after school, improving both his guitar and piano work becoming more important to him than good defensive action on the field.

His ambitions reversed, Maldwyn Pope is now looking forward to the release of his first album - on Rocket late this year - and his first concerts:

> "There is a Welsh thing, a longing for music, that's in the blood, I think. I just want people to listen to and enjoy my songs now because my songs are something I really enjoy myself.
>
> "They're all written from experience. I find it the easiest way to write. I know most older people laugh at me. My grandmother just tuts when she hears them and says "What do you know about love?". But young people don't seem to mind so much".

PENNY VALENTINE
Press and Publicity

CHAPTER 6

'Look what they've done to my song, ma!'

IT WAS PROBABLY BECAUSE I was so young, but I really don't think I was at all nervous about the recording sessions. I really felt completely at home with the whole process. One of the reasons Steve Brown had been late in giving us the arrangements for the recording week was that, at the last moment, the producer he had hoped would work on the new album pulled out. The new producer was David Costa, son of the legendary BBC broadcaster Sam Costa.

David was the perfect choice. He was very gentle and sympathetic but also treated me as a proper, grown-up artist. The first sessions were booked at the Mayfair Studios in South Moulton Street. The studio was really cutting edge and had just been upgraded from 8- to 16-track and was spread over a number of floors. The control room was on the first floor with the recording space on the floor above. Communication was achieved by the use of headphones and close circuit TV, which I thought was absolutely amazing.

I met the musicians for the first time that morning. It's strange now but I didn't really register the names of all of the musicians. I'm pretty sure the drummer on those sessions was Terry Stannard who played for a number of well-known Seventies bands, but all I remember about the bass player was that he had very long hair and a beard, which does absolutely nothing to narrow down the list of possible bass players living in London in 1973! They were very patient with my guitar playing which was probably not too bad but when it came to me playing piano, singing and keeping in time, it was thought best to bring in a professional. It wasn't too long until Nicky Hopkins turned up. He was your classic Seventies musician, long hair with a studio tan and just a little too thin to be really healthy. David Costa was very diplomatic because he thought I would possibly be upset to have the piano playing responsibilities taken off my shoulders. To be honest I couldn't have been more pleased. Even I knew that Nicky Hopkins had played with the Rolling Stones. As far as I was concerned, he was just another name to drop when I got back to school.

The session seemed to go pretty well. I would play the song to the band and then with David Costa's guidance, they would get it into some sort of shape and go for a take. When David was happy with the recording, I would then pop into the vocal booth and try for a vocal. It was all pretty quick and straightforward. I still remember seeing the jewel encrusted Fender Stratocaster guitar leaning against the wall of the vocal booth – we were sharing the use of the studio with Gary Glitter's band, which was at the time one of the biggest names in pop. Again more stories for the school yard.

Halfway through the afternoon David Costa asked me to pop down into the control room. A greetings telegram had just been delivered. I opened it with the eyes of everyone in the studio on me. It read:

GPO GREETINGS TELEGRAM

W21 GTG 4.10 LONDON T 20 GREETING =

MADWYN POPE C/O MAYFAIR SOUND STUDIOS 64 SOUTH MOULTON ST W1

VERY BEST WISHES FOR YOUR RECORDINGS LOVE ELTON +

I did notice that it was actually addressed to 'Madwyn Pope' rather than Maldwyn which showed that Elton was still having a bit of bother with my name, but in my eyes Madwyn was definitely a progression from Blodwyn Pig. What has to be remembered is that at the time, Elton was in the middle of the biggest rock tour of the USA to date – 40-odd venues across the country. The fact that he found time to make sure I felt welcome and wanted, made an incredible impression on me and I think gives an insight into his real character. In fact this was Elton at his most productive; he was contracted to write and produce two albums a year for Dick James. Every album seemed to improve on the last and each one sold more copies worldwide and especially in America. Add to that constant touring, especially in the US, and he really had the world at his fingertips.

The rest of my week followed a pretty regular pattern. Breakfast at the hotel, a full day in the studio recording, broken up by hamburger and chips at lunchtime, and out to some swanky restaurant in the evening where I'd order chips again. By now I had copies of all of Elton's albums to date, but was still waiting for his new double album *Goodbye Yellow Brick Road*. In fact, it was as we walked to breakfast one morning that I first heard the title track and fell in love with the song.

David Costa said he'd do some 'rough' mixes of what we had done so far and send them to me in Swansea. There was no white Rolls Royce for our return journey to Paddington station, but I didn't mind. I was going to go back to school on the following Monday and I couldn't wait to see everyone.

CHAPTER 7

'Back to life, back to reality'

GOING BACK TO SCHOOL was quite hard after being completely spoilt rotten during my time in London. I had recently moved from a small junior comprehensive school where I knew everyone, boys and girls, by their first names, to a boys only senior comprehensive school in the centre of town. We were the youngest in the school, the lowest of the low where every day felt like a fight for survival.

Dynevor had been a fine grammar school in its day and my mum had been to the girls' school which shared the site there before and during the war. We were the second intake for 'comprehensive' education and many of the teachers found the shock almost too much to take. They had been used to the well-mannered flower of Swansea youth hanging onto their every word during lessons – now they had to cope with a mixed rabble. I had gone to the new school in the company of most of my friends but to be honest I missed the girls. The school missed the girls. It had a different feeling to my old school and I missed it.

I wasn't exactly a target for any abuse or ill treatment but everyone knew about my record contract as it had now made it to the *South Wales Evening Post*. My saving grace was the football. I was still a member of the under-15 Swansea Schoolboys side, playing for the under-15s a year early and I used that to try to create some kind of 'hard guy, don't mess with me' persona. All of my real mates were kind of interested in my stories but within a couple of days we were all back to a new normality.

I think the whole process was helped by the greater success of one of my best friends, Jeremy Charles. Jeremy had great genes. His father was Mel Charles who had played for Wales and Arsenal and his uncle was the legend John Charles, who had played for Leeds and Juventus and was known as the gentle giant. I'd been in the same school or schoolboy representative team as Jeremy for three years – we even shared a lathe at woodwork lessons. As a young trainee teacher, my dad had taught Jeremy's dad Mel and even though the years had passed and Mel had gone on to great success in his footballing career, he always insisted on calling my dad Mr Pope.

I am reminded that during those years as the grammar school tried to cope with the changes, no teacher could be found to take charge of our school team. My dad was a regular fixture at our school games, always being ready to ferry three or four players to games across the city. Even though he wasn't really associated with the school, as a teacher he was able to take on the responsibility for the team and Mel would take on the tactical responsibility. At some games Mel would be joined by his brother John. I can still see my dad, barely five foot six inches being dwarfed by the Charles brothers. Looking back, any team that came up against us must have found that coaching team a pretty intimidating prospect and it might have had something to do with the fact that we were the most successful team in the city.

Whilst I had been swanning it in London, Jeremy had been on a week's trial at Everton. Elton John was fairly big news but a week at Everton did trump me and certainly helped to deflect some of the attention.

David Costa was always as good as his word and the tracks he sent down on cassette sounded pretty amazing to me. We had made a good start but more time was needed to record more songs for the album. Looking back now it does seem a strange way to run a business. I wasn't a great drain on the record label in terms of a weekly retainer which they would have paid to their other artists, but the recording bills were not insignificant with the sessions being booked at some of the newest and most expensive studios in London and the session musicians we used must have been fairly expensive too. At no time did the record company suggest that I should move to some sort of stage school. They were happy to work around my education commitments and wait until the next window of opportunity which I'm sure pleased my parents. Anyway the next trip was planned for later in the month to coincide with my half term holidays.

The next trip didn't just coincide with my half term holidays, it also coincided with my dad's. By the end of October my elder brother David was back in Cambridge, Gareth was studying for his exams which meant my dad would act as chaperone. It is strange – as kids, we can feel worried for our parents. Up until this point I'd been accompanied by my brothers, not my dad. He was an elder of my church, the Sunday school superintendent, a headmaster. What would he make of all that long hair and language in London?

Having said that I must say everyone who came into contact with me during my Rocket years was always very sympathetic to my tender age. They would always apologise for any slips they made with bad language. I still remember John Reid, Elton's manager, well known for his flashes of temper and for his ability to curse blushing after some four-letter tirade. Many years later I was told by a friend that prior to my first London trip, Steve Brown had gathered the whole record company together for a team talk about how they should treat me. Bearing in mind that this was the rock and roll industry of the 1970s, I really can't imagine all of the things Steve was worried about and it makes me laugh now that he took that headmaster's approach to his staff and colleagues. Having said that, I was in school and was as used to hearing as much profanity as any thirteen-year-old – but my dad, what would he think? It was only years later that I realised that my old dad had been in the navy for his war years, joining at nineteen. There was nothing he would hear or might see that he hadn't already experienced first-hand during those years and I'm sure it was that experience that made him so accepting of my new world.

The trip to London followed a very similar pattern with us setting up camp at the Cumberland Hotel and recording sessions either at the Mayfair or the CBS studio complex. The difference was my dad. He would talk to everyone. We would be sitting in the restaurant having breakfast and he'd strike up a conversation with whoever was near. It was late October and the weather was unseasonably warm. I still remember my dad starting a conversation with some unsuspecting US businessman as he tried to tuck into his bacon and eggs, commenting that this was an Indian summer. I felt so embarrassed; this wasn't Swansea or Pontrhydyfen where he'd grown up. This was London where people were on the go, rushing to a next appointment. But that was my dad and nothing was going to change him, and nothing ever has and the American really seemed to like having someone to talk to in a town that probably didn't have many people with the time for a chat.

The recordings went well but all week I was waiting for Friday. Elton's tour of the US had been incredibly successful and he'd been travelling non-stop from coast to coast. Steve had told me that he was flying in on the Friday and Elton was hoping to stop by and say hello. I knew that the last train to Swansea left at about nine o'clock and I was more concerned that Elton's plane would be late than whether the recordings went well.

My dad and I left the recordings studios at around sixish and made our way to the record company offices in Wardour Street. I still remember the excitement I felt when I saw a dark brown Phantom V Rolls Royce parked outside the front door. The offices were on two floors. The lower floor had the offices for John Reid's management company and the accountant Mr Rice and the top floor had the big room where I spent most of my time. I ran up the stairs, checked John Reid's office just in case Elton was there and then bounded upstairs to the main room. There he was, sat in his peacock wicker chair with big glasses and pink dyed hair. Even though by now it was early evening, the whole room was filled with the record company employees who had stayed late to witness the meeting.

I think that with all of the attention I got when I was in London, I was probably quite a cocky, chatty, precocious kid, but when I finally met Elton I was completely lost for words. Over the proceeding months, I had listened to and learnt all of his records. I had read every magazine article written about him, and here he was, having driven straight to the office from Heathrow airport, having completed the biggest US tour in rock history, to make sure he met me before I caught the train home to Wales, and I couldn't say a thing.

This is where my dad was such a godsend. Where he might have been slightly embarrassing to me, talking to complete strangers in our hotel, here he came into his own chatting to Elton about America, the travelling and in particular about some joint love affair with roses. I did manage to ask Elton to sign my autograph book. He wasn't sure what to put. Steve Brown suggested 'from one superstar to another'. In the end he chose to sign the book on the page opposite John Peel's autograph. It read:

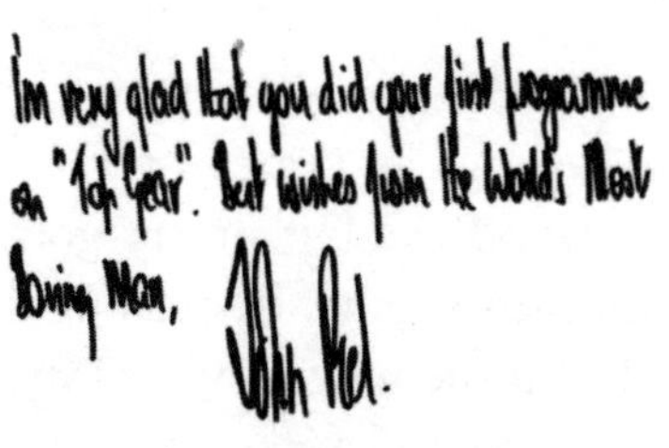

Best wishes to our next star! Elton John.

With that the time was gone and we had to get to Paddington once again. "We'll have to book a cab," my dad said. "Don't worry," said Elton, "take the Rolls," and with that my dad and me got into the Phantom V, waved goodbye to Elton and set off for the station and our second class seats reserved on the train back to Wales.

CHAPTER 8

'Step into Christmas'

I WAS STILL PLAYING football at this stage but it has to be said that it was starting to take a back seat in my priorities. Most of the time was filled with dreaming of the next trip to London and, when I wasn't doing my school work, the rest of the time still centred on the church. My friendships were also becoming more concentrated amongst my church friends, probably because culturally, in a world where teenagers were discovering alcohol etc., we were all the same in looking at the vices through the eyes of our parents and church leaders. Also, the football was more fun. The organised games were becoming more intense, competitive and aggressive and although I was never one to back down on the football pitch, I actually enjoyed playing the game rather than always feeling the need to win at any cost.

My next visit to London was planned for the end of the Christmas term. I was still writing songs and one of the new ones 'I Don't Know How to Say Goodbye' felt pretty good. With my brother David back from university, he was again given the duty of chaperone. I played the new song to David Costa and he immediately said we should record it. I was under the impression it was just a demo for the musicians to record on my next visit in the spring, so I recorded a simple guitar track and then a separate vocal. We also recorded a new song that I'd been working on with David. 'Hey Gunfighter' was a song influenced by a number of songs featured on the Elton John *Tumbleweed Connection* album. Bernie Taupin. Elton's writing partner had a special affinity with the Wild West with songs such as 'Ballad of a Well-Known Gun' and 'My Father's Gun':

> The man in black with a cigar in his hat and a six gun at his side...

As Penny Valentine said, I had been working on my piano-playing rather than my soccer and had come up with a fairly rocky piano part. David worked on the lyrics and again, when we got to the studio David Costa wanted to add the song to the album.

This was a great session for me because firstly, I got to play piano and secondly, I got to have a go at doing all of the backing vocals myself. With regards to the piano-playing it wasn't all plain sailing. The Christmas sessions had been moved from the Mayfair Studios to the relatively new CBS Studios in Whitfield Street. Mayfair might have been 16-track but it only had an upright piano. CBS had a massive studio and a giant grand piano which sounded amazing. The piano-playing was always going to be fairly exposed because I was playing on my own, without any click track to rely on or any other musicians to hide behind. Penny Valentine always said she loved the song because towards the end she could tell I was getting tired because the piano playing started to slow down. The session took place on Friday 21st December and the reason I know that is that I was presented with a section of two-inch recording tape which takes pride of place in my first and only scrapbook. The heading in the scrapbook says:

> This piece of tape was taken from a boob in the song 'Hey Gunfighter' Friday 21st December CBS. Dick took it out exactly.

After that, I put a lead vocal in and then continued to add harmony vocals to the choruses and then the odd 'ahh' section too, as the song developed. Up until this point I had been pretty blasé about what was achievable in the studio, but this really did seem like magic. At the time, people kept on saying my pre-pubescent voice sounded like Joni Mitchell, but listening back these days, maybe it was more like a chorus of chipmunks. However it sounded, I was hooked. In many ways again I think my church upbringing had prepared me for the harmony singing that would become so much a part of my musical future. In the little Gospel Hall back home, Sunday mornings were always a cappella. We did have a harmonium that my grandmother played and a piano for the Sunday school but Sunday mornings were instrument free. What that meant was that everyone and I mean everyone would sing the hymns in harmony. Someone would give out a hymn and one of the Francis brothers, either Uncle Dan or Uncle Harold, would pitch the tune. Uncle Jack was a very good bass singer and we all found a note somewhere above or below. I know pride is a sin but we were very conscious that our little fellowship had a very good reputation for its singing. So when David Costa suggested a harmony here or there, it seemed very natural to me.

We had to finish the session fairly early because Elton was in concert that night at the Hammersmith Odeon and we were going first to the gig and then to the after show party. This was the first year that Elton played a series of Christmas concerts in Hammersmith. He had opened the previous night, but this was the big one because everyone who was anyone would be there and would then go to the party. I had seen Elton in the office during the week and I had given him a Christmas card. I think this illustrates the strange position I was in. Here I was, travelling to London and recording my own songs in some of the finest recording studios in the world, mixing and chatting to the biggest recording artist in the world, and I had come to London with a home-made Christmas card which featured the Rocket Train logo with Watford on the first coach, Swansea on the second and Crystal Palace on the third because that was Steve Brown's favourite team. I had coloured the drawing in and stuck tinsel around the edges. It was straight out of *Blue Peter* rather than the *NME*. But I was never made to feel foolish or childish; Elton received the card with grace.

> *Elton John and friends*
> *invite you to a party*
> *immediately after*
> *his Hammersmith concert*
> *on Friday 21st December*
> *at*
> *7 Dials Studio*
> *31 Shelton Street*
> *Covent Garden*
> *London WC2*

This was also the first time I saw Elton's generosity. I'm pretty sure this was the year of the Sony Trinitrons, when all of Elton's colleagues and friends were given a colour television as a Christmas present. Penny Valentine was really up to her eyes with preparations for Elton's concerts when he presented her with her TV. She didn't really realise she had been quite so dismissive. Elton was quite upset and said, "If you don't like it I can get you something else". It was only then that she stopped to give him a kiss, when she saw how disappointed he had been by her lack of reaction.

With the session over, David and I hailed a cab to the Odeon and got there in time to see Kiki Dee open the show. We collected our especially reserved tickets and started star spotting from our great seats. To show the lack of fear I had and the delusions of grandeur I harboured, I remember very clearly sitting there all the way through her performance and thinking, "Hey, why didn't they ask me to do a couple of songs as well?" I might not have made the stage, but I did make the programme. Elton might still be on DJM Records but everyone associated with Elton was now working for Rocket. Clive Banks, the immaculate young promotions man, had an alter ego. Earlier in the year, he had sent out a hand-written note to a radio station and the reply came back addressed to Olive, rather than Clive. From then on Olive became the vehicle for a number of promotional devices. From a compilation album called *Olive's Choice* to an open-letter written for the programme from the fictional Olive, to her fictional mum telling her all the news from the new Rocket

Records Company. First mention in the letter goes to John Reid and Elton; the second mention is Kiki Dee and the third mention was about me:

> Then there's Maldwyn Pope, a 13-year-old Welsh singer-songwriter who's absolutely brilliant (none of your Donny Osmond's!).

This was my first Elton concert. In fact, it was my first ever concert and I knew every word to every song. When I got home I made a note in my scrapbook that 'Elton was brilliant'. Because it was Christmas he included 'Rudolph the Red-Nosed Reindeer' and finished off with 'Saturday Night's Alright for Fighting'. We even had fake snow to bring the show to an end, which Elton told me had got stuck in between the keys of his piano, meaning he couldn't play all of the notes.

David thought that with so many people at the gig, we might have trouble getting a cab so we made a sharp exit at the end of the concert to make sure we got to the party in Covent Garden in plenty of time. In fact we were one of the first to arrive, but not the first. Cradling a drink right in the centre of the massive room was a man straight out of our new song 'Hey Gunfighter'. He was all in black, skinny with a cowboy hat. I think he even wore a black poncho. David and I were given drinks by a very familiar-looking barman and kept ourselves to ourselves. The more I looked at the 'gunfighter' the more familiar he looked as well. I turned to David and said, "That's Cat Stevens!"

Eventually the party filled up with celebrity guests and it finally reached a crescendo with the arrival of Elton and his personal entourage. Elton went from guest to guest, making sure everyone was happy until he eventually found me. I told him how much I'd enjoyed the concert and then he asked me did I have my autograph book with me. I wasn't sure if it was cool or not to take it out, but I had brought it just in case. With that, Elton took it upon himself to make sure it was filled with as many names as possible. First he introduced me to Ringo Starr, and then we added all of the current top-line disc jockeys – Radio 1's Noel Edmonds, David Hamilton, Alan Freeman and Capitol's Gerald Harper.

Bryan Ferry was there accompanied by Brian Eno. Ferry was dressed in a Humphrey Bogart raincoat. He signed but didn't say much. Brian Eno was wearing make up and had painted fingernails, so I think we gave him a miss. Harry Nilsson was pretty much the worse for wear and wrote a minor epistle to go with his autograph. Micky Dolenz from the Monkees had crashed out on a cushion and Elton had to wake him up to get him into my book. The gunfighter man was Cat Stevens. He was quite close to Elton at this stage and they'd even recorded a couple of demos together and he was more than pleased to add 'Peace and Charity Cat Stevens' to my growing list. Finally, Elton marched me to the bar where he presented my autograph book to the barman. I took it back to find it had been signed by Graham Chapman from the Monty Python team who was helping to serve the drinks.

We got back to our hotel pretty late that night. The next day we caught the train home and then listened to Radio 1 as they broadcast Elton's Saturday night concert. As 1973 drew to a close it had been a truly remarkable year. With a new single, album and a series of concerts planned for 1974, the future looked incredibly bright.

Chapter 9

Biscuit factories and fast cars

THE NEW YEAR SAW David Costa work on the tracks in my absence as I tried to catch up on my school work. One of the songs seemed to be standing out as a potential single. Initially David had added piano. Bias Boshell was a member of Kiki Dee's band. He had often visited the studio during the recordings because he was a friend of David Costa's and I thought he was a lovely guy. Bias would go on to write 'I've Got The Music In Me' for Kiki but at this stage he was just another struggling musician looking for extra session work.

Many of the songs were having strings added but David had an unusual string system. On one visit to the studios, the PR man Clive Banks had threatened David Costa that if he didn't produce a hit he would have to add strings with one string player doing all the parts. David Costa then went on to tell him that's exactly how he did it. Some other sounds were added to the original track including a Celeste and Hammond organ and instead of the overdubbed solo string player a quartet was added. During the month we got a call from Steve Brown – everyone was so sure that the song was a hit that they had decided to add a whole string orchestral section. Steve also added that, because of the extra changes, the single was going to be put back from a January release to a release in March. As delighted as I was to hear about the orchestra, I was devastated by the delay in the releasing of the record. I think in the back of my mind I had the future completely mapped out. The single would be released, would be a hit and that would be the end of my regular school life. Although still convinced that a hit was on the cards, this meant that I had to endure another half term of school before it happened!

Although Steve Brown had taken a number of photos for early promotional work, it was felt that more were needed and instead of me going to London, Steve would send the photographer to me. Mike Ross had been responsible for a lot of the artwork for Elton's earlier work and, although he was still essentially freelance, he was still very much a part of the Rocket family and, together with his partner Lindi, was one of those familiar London faces to me. They decided to spend the weekend with us in Swansea as they looked for the images that would say I was a serious artiste. It was thought that my Welsh heritage should be reflected in the pictures. As it was winter in Wales you could pretty much guarantee the weather, but we set off looking for some industrial backdrop with me dressed in my school parka! We eventually settled on the British Steel works in Port Talbot. Michael snapped away until we noticed the arrival of the security guards. I'm not sure if they suspected industrial espionage or not but Michael's explanation that we were shooting an album cover fell on deaf ears and we were escorted to the main road and told not to return. Mike also took some pictures in the back garden against our old garage and all in all he seemed very happy with the results. (I was later told by Steve Brown that, although Mike Ross was an incredibly gifted art director, photographer and illustrator, he did have one flaw – he was colour-blind. Once, he created an illustration of Elton for a watch they were having made for promotional purposes. When Mike showed everyone his drawing they all laughed. He had given Elton green hair. Having said that maybe he was just being prophetic rather than colour blind!)

Come early March there was still work to be done on the album but we were now moving into promotion for the single 'I Don't Know How to Say Goodbye'. It was decided to have an official press launch and a room was booked at the Inn on the Park. A little PA system had been set up and I performed a number of songs as the press packs were handed out. Elton had been a regular guest on the London-based *Russell Harty Show* and the producer Mike Mansfield was in the small select group. It seemed to go quite well and Mansfield said he would be delighted to have me as a guest on the *Russell Harty Show*.

Penny Valentine had pulled in all the favours she had in the business and we started meeting people for lunch and interviews. The first was with Judith Simmons at the *Daily Express*. She was a well-respected writer, specialising in music and it was thought that the Beatles song 'Hey Jude' might have been written with her in mind. The lunch was fun. She and Penny swapped Beatles stories and we talked about my music, Wales and chapel. Just as we were about to leave, she asked me what were my hopes for the future. Quite off the cuff I said, "Well, I want to be a millionaire before I'm 18!" You can imagine what my parents said when they opened the *Daily Express* to see a picture of their cherub-like son with a headline 'Aiming for a Million':

> Maldwyn Pope is a 13-year-old with ambition – to be a millionaire by the time he is 18. And with his talent he could make it.

I remember when I got home one of the parents of my friends in the football team saying that he'd read the article in the *Express*. I was mortified and I'm sure I saw him snigger as he left me.

If the *Express* interview resulted in embarrassment the other interviews with the music press were surprisingly

Monday March 4 1974

Maldwyn Pope: Ambitious

Aiming for a million

MALDWYN POPE is a 13 year-old with an ambition—to be a millionaire by the time he is 18. And with his talent he could make it!

For last year this Swansea schoolboy sent a tape of himself singing one of his own compositions to disc jockey John Peel who was so impressed he featured Maldwyn on his radio show "Top Gear" . . . leading to a contract with Elton John's Rocket Records.

Next week Maldwyn has his first disc released, an adult-sounding ballad "I Don't Know How to Say Goodbye," to be followed by his first record album, also of his own compositions.

Maldwyn, whose miner grandfather wrote hymns, comes from a brainy family. His father is a head master, his mother also a teacher, his eldest brother David is at Cambridge University and elder brother Gareth studying for A levels.

positive. At the time, there were a lot of young singers finding success. Donny Osmond and Michael Jackson were topping the charts. *Opportunity Knocks* was throwing up new talent every week which seemed to come and go on that talent show conveyor-belt, but the fact that I had been discovered by John Peel, signed by Elton John and that I was writing my own material seemed to go down fairly well with the music hacks.

Whilst Penny Valentine was working the print media, Clive Banks was organising as much radio and television coverage as he could. A session was booked with John Peel which was broadcast on the 4th of March and featured the songs 'Maybe it's Wrong', 'Hey Gunfighter', 'All Day' and 'Autumn'. The main broadcasting outlets at this stage were Radios 1 and 2 and in London the newly-established independent station Capital. The single made *Roscoe's Round Table* and met with a favourable response, but it failed to make the all important Radio 1 playlist. It was all very well for the serious music press to delight in the fact that I was different to Donny and Michael, but the difference was that they made the playlist with every new release.

Nobody at the record company seemed too disheartened. After the initial media flurry, the next round of promotion was kept back until my Easter holidays in April. If the London radio stations hadn't been supportive of the single, it appeared that Manchester really seemed to take it to their hearts. Interviews had been arranged with BBC Manchester and the new independent station Piccadilly, because both had made the single 'record of the week'. It was decided that instead of driving to Manchester, Clive Banks and I would fly there for the day from Heathrow. Now this was the life I imagined.

This was the first trip to London I had made without a chaperone, but instead of being in a hotel alone I was welcomed into the homes of various people associated with the record label. Mostly I stayed with Steve Brown and his family but as I had to be at Heathrow first thing in the morning, I stayed at Schweppy's place the night before the flight. Stuart Epps or Schwepp, as everyone called him, had been a part of the Elton family from the early DJM days. It's funny how the smallest act of kindness can stay with you a lifetime. Everyone kept saying that my strange choirboy voice reminded them of Joni Mitchell, but in truth I'd never heard any of her music. Stuart mentioned this again one afternoon when I was in the Rocket office and it soon became apparent that I didn't know any of her music. He left and within half an hour he was back in the office with a copy of her latest album *Court and Spark* which he gave to me as a present and which I still have today. The following week I went to see Joni Mitchell at the New London Theatre where she was backed by Tom Scott and the LA Express band – the guys who would eventually come to worldwide attention with the theme music to *Starsky and Hutch*. The concert was great, made even more special by the fact that Steve Brown introduced me to George Harrison who we bumped into in the foyer. Anyway, Stuart lived not too far from Heathrow and it was his job to baby-sit me prior to the flight.

It was on that trip that I learnt a very valuable lesson. One of the DJs who interviewed me had recently moved to Manchester, after a few problems broadcasting in London. I can't for the life of me remember his name but one thing he said stuck with me. These days, there are a myriad of media outlets and answering the same questions can become repetitive and boring. But even back then by this stage, I had told my story many times to various journalists. What the DJ said was that I might have told the story a million times but for the interviewer it was the first and possibly only chance I would have to get my message across. He said I should remember to tell it with the same enthusiasm every time because that way every one benefited. The journalist got a good story and I got more coverage for my record.

One of the strangest interviews arranged by Clive was with UBN, The United Biscuits Network. There were so few independent radio stations that UBN became a regular drop off point for new artists looking to tell their story. United Biscuits made McVitie's biscuits, Jacob's Cream Crackers and Twiglets and had factories in Manchester, Glasgow and Liverpool. At their Osterley factory in London, they had built a radio studio which broadcast to their UK staff 24-hours-a-day. They mainly played top 40 material and survived on request from staff on the production line. "This one's for Maureen on Chocolate Biscuits!" As well as being a good opportunity for new artists, UBN also became the testing ground for a number of broadcasters, who would go on to national careers including Nicky Horne and Dale Winton. I remember turning up at the factory to be greeted by lots of people wearing white coats and hairnets. I don't think we were required to put on any special clothes but I do remember a very sweet, sickly smell in the studio. I had an interview and the record got played and we had spread the message to a very strange captive audience. We also came away with a couple of packs of biscuits!

That wasn't the only freebie Clive was responsible for putting my way that week. Clive knew that I always took my autograph book with me to the big parties. I think it had become something of a standing joke at the record company. It was during this week that Clive presented me with a very special present. I took a little red autograph book from him and started to thumb through the pages. Every major Seventies star had signed the book from Slade to the Osmonds. Ringo Starr had signed it and when I checked it against the one I had collected personally it was plain to see it was the real thing. Clive took the book off me to turn to a page he knew I'd be impressed with. He located the page with Mae West's flamboyant signature and then turned the page. There it was, 'Sincerely, Elvis Presley'. I almost fainted. He closed the book and said "it's for you". I couldn't believe it – firstly, that he'd given it to me and secondly, how he'd got hold of it. Clive had recently returned from Radio Luxembourg and he'd been given a pile of autograph books with the job of getting them signed by Elton and Kiki. The books were going to be special prizes in a Radio Luxembourg competition. He got Elton and Kiki to sign the books and he sent them all back, well, he sent them all back bar one! (And yes I've still got it!)

Those packets of biscuits came in handy as from the biscuit factory we headed west on the long road trip to Plymouth for my first television appearance. In 1974 there were very few programmes which gave an artist the opportunity to perform music for kids. *Young Eyes* was a new children's programme made for Westward TV. Clive Banks must have had a way with borrowing cars because for this trip he borrowed Bernie Taupin's Mercedes. The night before the broadcast we stayed at the Holiday Inn and I'm pretty sure Clive and I shared. The thing was that I might have been a kid at thirteen years old, but in truth most of the people working for the label were barely adults themselves. I think Clive must have been in his very early twenties – probably the same age as my brother David. We were having a great time; this was the best Easter holiday ever.

If I remember correctly, the show was live or if it was pre-recorded there was a live audience of kids in the studio. I was interviewed and then sang 'I Don't Know How to Say Goodbye' with just my acoustic guitar. I probably came across quite serious, but it was a hit with the kids. It was my first real experience of signing autographs. After the show, we had to rush back to London because I was due to meet up with Steve Brown. The journey from Plymouth to the M4 near Bristol seemed to take a lifetime and by the time we got to Bristol, Clive was a bit concerned that we might miss Steve in London. He decided to put his foot down and I'm pretty sure I saw the speedometer touch 140mph. It took us an hour to get back to London and it was the most exciting car ride I've ever had.

We met up with Steve and he seemed to be in quite a serious mood. He had been in a meeting with the rest of the Rocket directors about the future of the label. I think Steve was concerned that, although the label was supposed to be fun and idealistic for all those involved, for him it was a full-time commitment. As the other directors weren't involved on a day-to-day basis, they were able to stand on the sidelines and criticise. Up until this point, the only real success the company had had was Kiki Dee's 'Amoureuse'. The label had been funded with an advance from MCA in the US, but the money wouldn't last forever. Elton was still tied into DJM for a number of albums so he wouldn't be a ready source of income for some time to come. In the end, it was decided to have a cull of the label roster. Steve said I wasn't to worry, everyone was in agreement that they should retain me and Kiki Dee. Even as a teenager, I realised from the way Steve was talking that things weren't right.

It also became apparent that not every one was happy with the direction my album was taking. Record producer Gus Dudgeon was also one of the founding directors of Rocket and it was decided that he would play a more active role in the record label and in particular with my future recordings. All of this would develop more over the coming weeks and months, but I was still having a ball and I was especially looking forward to the next few days because I'd been invited to stay at Elton's house in Virginia Water.

CHAPTER 10

Subbuteo football and Watford FC

THE EXCITEMENT OF STUDIO recording, TV and radio shows and flights to Manchester paled into complete insignificance compared with going to stay at Elton's house. I think it was Steve Brown who took me and I remember we had to wait for the electric gates to open before we could drive up to the front door. Outside the house sat the brown Phantom V a Ferrari, a Rolls Corniche Convertible and a Mini complete with minibar and TV!

It's often been said that Elton is a big kid at heart and his home certainly reflected that. The house was a very big open-plan bungalow. There was the obligatory swimming pool and Steinway grand piano but the best thing of all was the play room. The walls were covered in gold and platinum records and there were Grammy awards displayed in cabinets. That was all very well but the best bits were the games machines. He had the arcade tennis game, pinball machines and a bar football 'foosball' table just like the one they had at the camp site at Poppit Sands, and we just played. He was brilliant at the 'foosball' and thrashed me. Then he got out his Subbuteo football set, a game where the players are mounted on little stands and you flick them against a plastic football. It would be a little while before I met Elton's lovely mum Sheila and his stepdad Derf, but I could tell what sort of man Derf was when Elton told me that he had actually made models of terraces and football stands to add realism to Elton's Subbuteo set. Elton had a team painted in Watford colours and I had the other team.

If Elton was good at 'foosball' he met his match with me that night when it came to Subbuteo. I beat him three goals to two, although I think he thought it rather unfair that I didn't wait for him to prepare his goalkeeper at one stage in the game, before taking a shot. After we'd had something to eat, we jumped into Elton's Roller and drove over to meet another of the Rocket Records directors. Compared to my house in Swansea, Bernie Taupin's house was a mansion but compared to Elton's house it seemed, well, rather small. If the house wasn't overly impressive, the welcome I got from Bernie and his wife Maxine was wonderful. Bernie had met Maxine during one of Elton's tours of the US and she was the inspiration for the song 'Tiny Dancer' they both wrote. Bernie was really interested in my songs and even brought out a book of children's poems he had written. Writing lyrics is a very special talent and Bernie was abundantly blessed with this gift. Elton could always write great tunes but without the lyrics Bernie wrote first, which provided the tempo template that became Elton's hits, it has to be wondered how successful Elton would have been. The highlight of the evening for me was phoning home and hearing Elton and Bernie talking to my brother Gareth back in Swansea. Two worlds colliding!

Elton has also been known for his love of collecting and it seemed as though every corner of the house had some incredible knick-knack that he'd fallen in love with on his travels. There were paintings, stuffed animals and sparkling jewels. The guest room I stayed in was full of metal cases which held his various glasses. The platform shoes were stacked in layers and on the wall were the Andy Warhol prints of Marilyn Monroe. Back home I was still sharing a bed with my brother – here I was staying in a room which was worth millions. Elton made sure I had a glass of water for the night and explained that if I did need anything I would have to wake him up because the burglar alarm was set for the rest of the house. I was thinking to myself this can't get any better, but do you know what, the next day it did.

Elton said that we had to be up early the next morning for our daytrip. As usual, the excitement of the secret seemed to give him a great deal of pleasure. Elton was dressed in the same outfit that he would wear on the cover of his next album *Caribou*. It was a tiger skin bomber jacket and oversized rose-tinted glasses. We jumped into his Rolls Corniche Convertible and lying on the seats was a couple of enormous towels embroidered with the word Superstar. I thought we can't be going swimming because he's got a pool in the back garden. As we travelled on this mystery trip, Elton played a copy of Paul McCartney's album *Band on the Run*. At one point, he stopped the car and turned the volume up. He wanted to point out some out of tune guitars on the song 'Bluebird'. Elton couldn't believe that they had let it slip through. I was still wondering where we were going when Elton turned the massive car down a small street in Watford and we stopped outside Vicarage Road, the home of Watford FC. A life-long fan of football and the club, Elton had become president of the club the previous year and took his role seriously, attending as many matches as possible, mentioning the team in every interview he could and also training with the team when time permitted. By taking me to a morning training session, I was joining a fairly select group which also included his friend, rock rival and former Brentford FC apprentice Rod Stewart. I must admit I thought I had been the only one to join him at one of these sessions but, in an article written for *Rolling Stone* magazine sometime later, Paul Gambaccini named me and Rod Stewart as having been guests at these training sessions. We took part in all of the activities – running, shooting and taking penalties. We even took our turn to head the ball towards the goal from the manager's crosses, which was a little awkward for Elton as he was still wearing his large glasses. I can't imagine what these full-time professional footballers thought. Elton had told them about my being the captain of Swansea Schoolboys but the event must have been something they took for granted, having a celebrity rock star associated with their club. I don't think I did too badly, but just like Elton, they all seemed to have problems with my name and it ended up with everyone calling me Kevin for most of the morning.

The day really was one of those 'Jim'll Fix it' moments. On the way back to Virginia Water, we listened to Radio 1 and tuned in just in time for the lunchtime quiz. Right on cue the DJ asked, "In which year did Elton John have a hit with 'Your Song'?" Elton shouted at the radio "1970". I turned to him as the clock ticked down the time for the contestant to answer and said, "Elton wasn't it 1971?" "1971," said the DJ. Elton might have lived his life but I'd read all about it and knew the times and dates of almost every release and every hit record.

The rest of the week was filled with interviews for some of the smaller regional papers and travelling back and forth to Steve Brown's house in Lenham, Kent. The following week I was due to have another special treat. Elton always wanted to share the good time he was having with his friends, and with Watford playing at home, I was to join a rather odd bunch who had also been invited to the game. John Reid, Elton's manager had also become a director of Watford and he was in charge of the travelling arrangements for us to get to the game where we would join up with Elton in the director's box.

The trip would be made in two Rolls Royce cars travelling in convoy. You must remember that, although I was mixing regularly in these circles, the rest of my life was back in school in Swansea. At times I would have to pinch myself that all of this was happening and sometimes I would actually find the whole thing a little embarrassing too. One of the key members of the party was Tony King. He had been general manager of the Beatles, owned Apple Records and had become very friendly with Elton when he first started making an impact in Los Angeles. Tony looked absolutely magnificent in his baker boy, *Great Gatsby* hat and long, checked coat. Also making the trip were two ladies, also from the music business, whose names I didn't catch, but one piece of information I gleaned and has stayed with me ever since was that one of them was responsible for the Hollies having a hit with 'The Air That I Breathe'. The fact that they wore very big, thick fur coats only added to the glamour of the event. On the way from Soho to Watford, John Reid decided he needed something to eat, so both cars pulled up on the pavement outside a chip shop and this strange group of people all trooped out of the limousines to order fish and chips which they ate out of the paper, sitting on the Roller's leather seats.

We got to Watford and John Reid organised our way to the director's box. I think we must have looked extremely odd but everyone there seemed to be used to this type of thing. One of the ladies was carrying a hamper. It was a typical cold evening match and halfway thought the first half, she opened the hamper, spread a tartan shawl on our laps and then proceeded to serve us all Irish coffee from a thermos flask. I know Dorothy had a hard time getting used to Oz, but I must admit I was getting pretty freaked out in Watford!

CHAPTER 11

The BBC, 32 Alexandra Road, Swansea

AFTER THE EXCITEMENT OF staying at Elton's home and all of the interviews I had done to promote the single, getting back to real life was quite hard. The routine of school, football and church did help to put some shape to my life, but I had the showbiz bug now and I couldn't wait to release a new single, finish the album, and start touring. There had been talk of maybe supporting Kiki Dee at the Fairfield Hall in Croydon or maybe even going to America. The first single hadn't been a hit, but everyone was still very positive.

It was around this time that I had my first contact with BBC radio in Wales. With the record release getting quite a lot of national coverage, I was contacted by Anita Morgan from the BBC in Wales. Anita was a radio reporter based at the Swansea BBC studios and she would send reports up to Cardiff to be used in a morning show presented by Vincent Kane. This was still a number of years before the start of BBC Radio Wales. It was on that day in 1974 that I fell in love with a building. I didn't have far to go because Dynevor School was just down the road from the BBC, but as I walked in through the doors of 32 Alexandra Road for the first time to record an interview, I knew that this was a special place for me.

I think I was expecting the studios to be at least as well equipped and staffed as the biscuit factory, but I was soon to realise the place had seen better days. Most of the studio and office space wasn't being used, and in fact Anita recorded the interview in a disused office on the second floor on a portable Nagra reel to reel tape recorder. Well it was just about portable, although it did have the ability to almost dislocate your shoulder if you weren't up to the job! After we had finished the recording, Anita showed us around and it was the first time I saw the concert hall size studio which, in truth, was gradually falling apart. Anita obviously loved the studios as well and she explained how in the glory days of the building the three studios on the second floor had been linked together. The smallest studio was for the producer who could see through strategically placed windows both the concert studio and the smaller and more intimate drama studio. At the appropriate time, he could cue the conductor to start the music and then direct the actors to start their performances, while he sat with the engineer mixing the sound together.

The drama studios were also legendary in their own right. Dylan Thomas had been a regular broadcaster from that room and I always felt something of his presence when I entered that room. In fact, there are a number of photographs of Dylan in front of a microphone from that studio and also pictures of him with friends Vernon Watkins and Daniel Jones in the room together. I always thought that it would be great if one day it could be restored to its former glory, and many years later I was fortunate enough to see that dream come true. In many ways seeing this jewel of a building with a great story within the bricks and mortar to boot, was the first catalyst in inspiring me to take the stories of people and places from my home and take them to a wider audience. The interview was played out one morning and we all sat around the radio at home before going off to school. The interview finished with them playing a part of the single. I remember the legendary Welsh broadcaster Vincent Kane back-linking the interview in typical fashion. "Fourteen-year-old schoolboy Maldwyn Pope with 'I Don't Know How to Say Goodbye'. Well, he's hardly had time to say hello!"

Even though I was yet to record my first hit record, I still had plenty of people championing my music. One in particular was the broadcaster and journalist Paul Gambaccini. I first met Paul at the BBC when I went to record a second session for John Peel's *Top Gear* show. At the time, he was studying Politics, Philosophy and Economics at Oxford University but during his time studying in America he had become involved in university radio and by doing so found his true vocation. Whilst in the UK he had started writing for *Rolling Stone* magazine and in 1973 interviewed Elton for the paper. John Peel's producer, John Walters read the article and saw the potential that Gambaccini had and invited him to broadcast on Radio 1. Paul was a unique voice on the station bringing a depth of knowledge, a breadth of vocabulary together with a love for pop music that was only enhanced by his American accent. It was around the time of the release of the single that Paul first interviewed me for the *Friday Night Rock Show*. I thought Paul was fantastic, slightly odd and geeky, but just so much fun. He was just so quirky he used to make me laugh. Sometimes it seemed he would have a whole conversation on his own, where we'd all just be listening in on him interviewing himself.

As well as writing for *Rolling Stone* Paul was much in demand for music and mainstream publications. In one of his many articles he said that although 'I Don't Know How to Say Goodbye' hadn't been a hit, it was destined to become a valuable copyright. He believed in the song so much so that, when the Williams Twins came to town, he gave them a copy of the record and told their manager that they should cover it. The Williams Twins were the latest teeny bop sensation to be exported to Britain from the US. They were the twin nephews of legendary singer and TV show host Andy Williams, who had been also been responsible for the early success of the Osmonds. These identical blond twins had it all, the looks, the voices and the connections. The keyboard player from Toto, David Paich, was given the job of producing the track and when it was released, it just about scraped into the Billboard

Hot 100. Another artist called Corelia also charted with the same song in South Africa. The song wasn't exactly a great money spinner, but it was a major confidence booster to me and to everyone at Rocket, showing there was real interest in the music whether it was recorded by me or someone else.

With all of this excitement, it might have been possible to ignore the obvious, but something was starting to happen to me in 1974. Nature was starting to take its course. The choirboy voice that had been so much a part of my original sound was starting to fall. Not in great leaps as some voices fall – it was just a little lower every day. Also, the misgivings about the original album expressed by record producer and Rocket Records company director Gus Dudgeon were also coming to a head. Steve had challenged the other original directors to be more involved in the record company and Gus decided to take up that challenge by taking responsibility for me.

It was rather difficult because no one told me that I wouldn't be working with David Costa anymore and I'm sure David must have felt quite hurt that he was being sidelined. After a meeting with Gus and singing a couple of new songs I had written to him, the decision was made. It was too late to work on the old recordings because of the change in my vocal range. That album would be scrapped and we would start again. I must admit it was around this time that I started to have some doubts about this music business. Up until this moment the future had seemed pretty well mapped out: record some songs, have a hit, tour a bit, leave school and then I would achieve that ambition of being a millionaire before I was 18. Now it didn't seem quite so straight forward, although having said that, I was now going to work with the most successful record producer on the planet, so maybe we were back on track after all!

Gus Dudgeon was just perfect, exactly how I imagined a big time record producer should be. He was always dressed immaculately and the one thing I always remember about Gus was that he always smelt expensive! He had come up through the recording studio ranks, starting his career as a tea boy at Olympic Studios before progressing from tape op to producer. He had picked up the production job on David Bowie's single 'Space Oddity', because Tony Visconti, Bowie's regular producer, didn't like the acoustic guitar demo. After producing Elton's first album *Empty Sky*, Steve Brown told Elton he wasn't the right man for the job and that they would have to find a 'proper' producer. They had approached the Beatles producer George Martin but for various reasons it didn't work out. In reality Gus got the job offer by default. Gus told me he knew as soon as they approached him that he was going to take Elton on, but he made them wait just long enough before he said yes, just to make them worry, and play a little hard to get.

Gus got all of the original album tapes and also got me to record any new songs for him to listen to. It was at Gus's instigation that I got my first multi track tape recorder. It was an Akai 4000DS reel to reel tape machine, which allowed you to bounce from one track to another. Although it was a major breakthrough for me, it was pretty basic technology and it did mean that if you got the overdub wrong, you had to start again. But for me, it was just the most fantastic toy. With piano, organ, guitar, tambourine and vocals I got my first self-taught lessons in record production. Gus chose six songs for the first session and I couldn't wait to start.

The sessions were booked in the Marquee Studios which were at the back of the legendary Marquee Club, just up the road from the Rocket Offices in Wardour Street. The start of the first session was delayed because they were upgrading from 16- to 24-track and they were still wiring in the machinery right up to the last minute. As well as having the most successful record producer in the world, I was also going to have some of the most successful musicians playing on the recordings too. In fact, these sessions were almost a dry run for a new Elton John band line-up. Joining these sessions were Roger Pope on drums and Freddy Gandy on bass. This rhythm section had played together for years in another DJM band called Hookfoot, named after the strange way Roger used to hang onto some of his drums as he played. Some websites actually say that Roger Pope was my dad, but the surname was just a coincidence. On guitar was Davey Johnstone from Elton's current band. Davey was a tall, gangly, long-haired blond Scotsman who could play just about any stringed instrument. Gus had met him whilst producing a folk band called Magna Carta and he had really made a difference to Elton's studio and live sound ever since. He arrived with nothing short of an articulated truck carrying all of his instruments from a Les Paul Black Beauty 3 Pickup guitar to a mandolin and sitar! Completing the line-up was the keyboard player Mike Moran who is probably best known for representing Britain some years later in the *Eurovision Song Contest* singing 'Rock Bottom' with Lynsey de Paul. I didn't know much about Mike, but on one track I said I'd really like a similar feel to a song called 'Gonna Make You an Offer You Can't Refuse' by a guy called Jimmy Helms – did he know it? Did he know it! He'd played piano on that track as well.

We went through a similar process to the ones we'd had on the David Costa sessions. I would play the song to the band, either on piano or guitar, and then they would kick it around for a bit. Then Gus would work his magic.

When making Elton's records Gus had Elton's complete trust. Often Elton would be there for the initial tracking sessions. He would do a number of vocal takes and some backing vocals and then he would let Gus get on with it. I think this was partly due to the incredible workload that Elton was under. Contractually, he had to write and record his two albums a year and after recording one, he would be touring with that until the new album was released. For the first few Elton albums that he produced, Gus wasn't even hindered by having to use Elton's band, as it was thought it would be better to use seasoned studio musicians for the records and let Elton's band grow into their roles by doing the live work.

Gus would commission the strings, backing vocals and overdubs. Gus didn't have any real formal musical training, but he knew what he wanted to hear on a track from the various sections. For example, sometimes he would sing the parts he heard the brass playing to an arranger, who would then score out the lines for the session musicians to play. Eventually, he would present Elton with up to three different mixes of each track. Elton then gave his preference and that would be the finished track on the album.

In many ways I was more fortunate than Elton in seeing Gus working on a track. For my recordings, I was booked for the whole of the school holiday, so even when I wasn't needed I would still be there for the overdubbing sessions too. Gus had a strange way of working. If you were a casual observer, you might not have really been able to see what he was actually bringing to the party. Initially, a lot of time was spent with everyone in the control room drinking tea. Gus would hold court telling great stories about other sessions he'd worked on. Sometimes these would go on for an hour or so before he'd say, "Right, is everyone ready for a take". By this time, he'd created such a great atmosphere in the studio, the tracks sounded really fresh and fun. The sessions would last into the early hours and then a limousine would pick me and Gus up and take us to Gus's house, where we would sleep in late before going over the same process again the next day. Gus's wife was a lady called Sheila who I think was part-Brazilian. She was a very sweet and welcoming lady and again full of stories. Steve Brown once said that she had invited him and his wife Gill to dinner once and he rang during the day to remind her that he was vegetarian, but not to go to any particular trouble on his account. When she served the dinner that night everybody got a lovely roast and he got a plate of Brussels sprouts!

I loved the daily car rides in and out of the studio because Gus would just keep telling me story after story. I remember after one session, he turned to me and said, "Maldwyn, I wish I was you; you have such an amazing future ahead of you." I didn't know what to say, but I thought to myself, well maybe I won't be in school too much longer after all.

The first track we recorded was a song called 'When You're Away'. Davey had his Les Paul guitar and started playing a single note over a really pounding backing track. I just felt like a million dollars. I think I just smiled and smiled whilst they laid down this amazing rock track. As always, I kept thinking what's everyone going to say back home when they hear this.

Gus and Davey wanted me to play as much acoustic guitar as possible on the tracks, which was a great encouragement to me and everything really started to come to life when Davey started adding all of his overdubs. He could literally play any stringed instrument and, what I always marvelled at, was his enthusiasm and his ability to come up with idea after idea. The tracks were soon filled with mandolins and assorted electric and acoustic guitars and I thought they sounded like finished masters, but I should have known better, Gus was only just getting started.

At this stage in his career, Gus was the most successful record producer in the world and was able to call on just about anyone to ask them to contribute to his productions. When it came to string arrangements, Gus called on Richard Hewson. Hewson had an amazing track record, having written the string arrangements for The Beatles' 'Long and Winding Road' and 'Let it Be'. I think Gus was trying him out to see if he would be good for some future recording for Elton. Hewson was aware of that as well and consequently he came up with stunning arrangements for all of the tracks.

When it came to backing vocals, Gus heard a Beach Boys type of arrangement for a song called 'Everything I've Got'. This was around the time of 'Don't Let the Sun Go Down on Me' where a number of the original Beach Boys sang back-up vocals. When it became too difficult to get hold of them for my tracks, he turned to a band called First Class who had had a Beach Boys sound-alike hit called 'Beach Baby'. Again the results were stunning. Gus did a lot of this extra work whilst I was back in school, so I had to wait until my next school holidays to hear the results. I returned to London and the Marquee Studios just before Christmas to contribute some extra vocals. Gus's master plan was to come up with a couple of hit singles and then, in the New Year, carry on with the recordings for the rest of the album.

I can laugh now at my innocence because there must have been so many things going on around me that I just didn't understand. To illustrate the point, I remember a number of conversations in the studio where various people were described as being 'a friend of Dorothy'. I couldn't believe Dorothy had so many different friends. Now I was inquisitive by nature, and I expect slightly precocious in these surroundings because people were treating me as someone special. So, after this phrase had been used a number of times, I asked what for me was the obvious question, "Who's Dorothy?" I didn't understand why it made everyone in the room laugh. No one at the time explained that it was a gentle way of referring to someone's hidden sexuality and for years I wondered who that Dorothy was. Even now it brings a smile to my face.

It was around this time that I was in the presence of musical history and I almost missed it because I fell asleep on a couch at the back of the studio. Elton had become friendly with John Lennon, having been introduced by the same Tony King, who had been at the Watford game. One night in New York, when John Lennon was recording some new tracks, Elton dropped by the studio and ended up singing and playing piano on 'Whatever Gets You Thru' the Night'. Lennon had based the original idea on George McRae's disco hit 'Rock Your Baby', and thought the song fairly ordinary and run-of-the-mill. When Elton added his piano part and some harmony vocals, he became convinced that the song would be a hit. Lennon was still unconvinced so when Elton made a bet with him that if he was right and it went to number one, Lennon would have to appear on stage with him. John felt pretty sure that his performing days weren't in danger of returning anytime soon. Well, Elton's commercial judgement was proved right and the song went to the top of the Billboard charts. Of course Elton called in the bet and John was a guest at his Thanksgiving Day concert at Madison Square Gardens.

By any standards, this was going to be a momentous event. Lennon hadn't performed live for some time and Davey Johnstone once told me that Lennon was so nervous, he found him throwing up in the toilets before the concert. At this time, Elton was the biggest rock star on the planet and there had been rumours in New York all day that Elton would be joined by a very special guest. When the crowd realised the man walking onto the stage in sunglasses was Lennon, they erupted. It was a special night for Lennon on a number of levels. The reaction of the crowd showed how much he was loved and how much he was missed. Also, when he came offstage, he found Yoko Ono waiting for him and after being separated for some time, this marked the start of their reconciliation. Lastly, the concert became even more poignant due to the fact that Lennon's contribution would be his last public performance.

The concert was both filmed and recorded and the tapes were couriered over from the United States for Gus to mix. I think at this stage there were no definite plans of what they were going to do with the tracks, but I remember Gus being so excited when he heard the tracks were in the country.

The trouble was that we had been working all day and when my time was over, Gus just carried on. He knew what an important piece of musical history he had in his possession and he didn't want me to miss out. I remember on the tape that John introduced the final track by saying he wanted to thank Elton and the boys and he wanted to do one more song before he left the stage to be sick. The song he closed with that night seemed an odd choice. The breakdown in relations between Lennon and Paul McCartney was well-documented, but he chose to perform a song he'd never sung with the Beatles. He slightly stumbled on his intro as he described it as a song written by an old estranged fiancé of his called Paul, and with that, they kicked into 'Saw Her Standing There'. When I heard it, I just couldn't believe that I was in such a privileged position. In future years, when I've been asked to perform a cover or when I've been out playing with my band the Jacks, I always include the song and it always reminds me of that special time with Gus.

Chapter 12

'He's a Pinball Wizard'

One event in this year probably sums up the difficult emotional tightrope I was walking. It became my routine that, during every school holiday, I would travel to London to spend some time at the record label offices whether I was recording or not. On one trip to London I was told by everyone that, the following day, I was going to have a very special treat. A taxi was booked to pick me up and take me to a secret destination.

I was dropped off outside a building and told to go and ring the bell. I gave my name to the lady on reception and she said I was expected. I walked into the main recording room at Eel Pie Studios to be greeted by a scene out of Madame Tussauds. The room was full of faces I recognised from the world of film and rock. The event was the recording of Elton's 'Pinball Wizard' for the new Ken Russell film. Elton's friend Rod Stewart had recorded the Pete Townshend song in 1972 and when the idea of a film based on the rock opera was first mooted, Rod Stewart was approached to sing the song and appear in the movie. He asked his mate Elton John what he thought, and Elton told him not to touch it with a bargepole. A couple of years later, with Ken Russell now in the role of director, Elton was approached with the request to take on the role which Rod had turned down. Elton said yes immediately and it's said that Rod found it hard to forgive him for some time.

And so it was that I was invited to be a spectator at the recording session. One of the first things that struck me was Keith Moon's eyes. Keith Moon was the troubled drummer of The Who, well-known for his eccentric and ultimately self-destructive behaviour. His eyes seemed to stare at everything and everyone and I kept thinking to myself, I wonder why he's so cross. Pete Townshend, the man who wrote 'Pinball Wizard' was acting as mediator, trying to keep the peace between the various different egos in the room. One of those strange, small details I remember is that Townshend wore a tank top with the name Pete Townshend repeated as the pattern, which I think had been made by his wife on a knitting machine.

Although he was the film's director, Ken Russell took a bit of a back seat; the man in charge was Gus Dudgeon. Gus was at the top of his game and wasn't going to play second fiddle to anyone when it came to recording. I was given a seat which was next to the window which looked down onto the piano booth where Elton sat. He wore the same tiger skin bomber jacket and pink-tinted glasses that he wore on the front cover of the *Caribou* album and I remember Elton being a little nervous. The day was just a dream. I remember Elton's fingers flying over the keys as he played the piano figure at the start of the track. I remember the whole studio staring at Elton as he sang his lead vocal, standing alone with a glass of whisky in his hand. Occasionally Gus would turn to Pete Townshend and Ken Russell to check, but in many ways this was Gus's gig more than Elton's. This was rock 'n' roll history and I was there to see it first hand.

As 1974 drew to a close I reflected on what had been a very exciting but strange year, where I had been privy to some great musical moments and also party to some of the decisions that went on behind the scenes. Elton's follow up album *Caribou* had not been as successful as *Goodbye Yellow Brick Road*. That was hardly surprising, as they only had just over a week in between touring commitments to record the whole thing. Even the artwork was a rush job. For *Goodbye Yellow Brick Road*, there had been time to create an iconic image, but for the new album they used some fairly straightforward photos of Elton for the cover. I remember Steve had the job of helping to decide the name for the record. Never one to take himself too seriously, Elton wanted at one stage to call the album 'Old Red Eyes Is Back,' a title quickly vetoed by Steve. In the end the name of the studio became the name of the album *Caribou*. Steve was given an acetate of the album to listen to and the first time I heard 'Don't Let The Sun Go Down On Me' it became one of my favourite Elton songs. The next morning I couldn't wait for Steve to come down to breakfast. "I just love that song," I told Steve. "Yes," he said, he knew. He'd heard me play it a dozen times in a row as he lay in bed trying to catch some sleep before going back to the office.

The year ended with a Christmas trip to London. This was the first time I noticed that Elton was walking around the offices carrying a bottle of spirits. It never seemed to leave his sight. He had bought all of his close friends Christmas presents but even those had been a bone of contention. Most of them had been bought Rembrandt etchings but there weren't enough etchings to go around, so he had to buy Steve Brown an original Salvador Dali oil painting. In the court of Elton John some people found that favouritism hard to take.

CHAPTER 13

I'm sorry Steve Brown doesn't work here anymore...

THE YEAR 1975 WAS strange. It started very brightly with a mention in *Cosmopolitan* magazine. Anne Nightingale was the only female broadcaster on BBC Radio 1 and she wrote a regular column for *Cosmo* called 'Cosmo Listens to the Records'. I'm not sure how a copy came to our attention, because it wasn't a regular magazine in our Swansea circles, but I still have a copy of the article in my scrapbook. The page featured reviews of the new albums by John Lennon, Randy Newman, Rod Stewart and The Who but tucked in there amongst the superstars she wrote:

COSMO LISTENS TO THE **RECORDS**

by Anne Nightingale

As someone who doesn't enjoy the child-promotion that's gone on to make Lena Zavaroni a cabaret star before she'd normally be old enough to sit in the audience—there *is* one worthwhile prodigy I'd nominate: Maldwyn Pope, a fourteen year old schoolboy from Wales who has written and recorded, but is taking "O" levels rather than auditions for the time being. He isn't left a lot of time for the exhausting business of promoting himself into a star. Conveniently, the very career-conscious nephews of Andy Williams—the professionally groomed Williams Twins—have now recorded one of Maldwyn's songs, *Don't Know How To Say Goodbye*. Maldwyn's talent lies not in precociously trying to express sophisticated emotions, but in writing simply and beautifully. His first album, due out soon on the Rocket label, will be produced by Gus Dudgeon. *He* was the man behind the first hits of David Bowie and Elton John . . . so take not my word, but Mr Dudgeon's, that Maldwyn is going to be phenomenal.

The year continued with trips back and forth to London, staying with Gus, recording and trying to maintain a normal school life as well. I was still playing a lot of football and doing a lot of church but I think my head had been turned and everything other than the music felt a bit ordinary. Gus was in great demand as a producer.

I suppose even I could read between the lines that Steve Brown wasn't completely happy with the way the record company was working out, but I wasn't prepared for the news I was about to receive. I remember coming back from school checking with my mum to see if it was OK to use the phone and calling the Rocket number. "Can I speak to Steve please," I said. "I'm sorry, he doesn't work here anymore," said a voice I didn't recognise. At that moment I felt my new world start to crumble. I don't think I cried, but I was very close. Steve wasn't just the boss of the record company – he was becoming the most important adult figure in my life apart from my parents. He seemed to be so in charge of everything and could make anything happen. Now he wasn't there anymore. Not only had Steve left, Clive Banks had been head-hunted to be head of promotions at Island Records and Penny Valentine had decided to go back to journalism. Everything was changing and as far as I was concerned it was changing too fast.

It took some time for me to make contact with Steve because he refused to answer the phone to anyone. One day he had been driving into the office at Wardour Street from his home in Kent and met a very big traffic jam. He thought about the job and he thought about the future and he thought about the lack of support he felt he was getting from the other directors of the record company. So he decided to turn the car around, drive home and never go back. At this stage, Steve was an independently wealthy man. He had been there at the start of Elton's career. Elton still referred to him as the 'original mentor' whereas Steve always referred to his artist friend as 'Reg-Elton'. Steve had produced Elton's first album and co-ordinated all of the others up to *Caribou*. Every sale resulted in a small proportion finding its way to Steve, and Elton sold an awful lot of albums. I was told by one of Steve's brothers that the wealth didn't always sit well with Steve and, that at one stage, he bought a number of tractors which were given to farmers in Africa. Anyway, he was gone and I was bereft.

It wasn't too long before things became clearer. An old friend of Elton's, by the name of David Croker, was brought in to take over from Steve. David had had experience running the Bell record label and it was he who had introduced John Reid to Elton a number of years earlier. It was always going to be difficult for me to accept someone trying to step into Steve's shoes but David made me feel very welcome and tried to reassure me that I was still going to be a priority at Rocket Records. The first time we went out for lunch together, he presented me with a book about the Marx Brothers because he knew I was a big fan.

The departure of Steve Brown did cause a number of problems. My first loyalty was with Steve and he became my de facto manager and mentor. The trouble was he wasn't speaking to any of the other directors of the company including Gus. Elton would ring leaving long messages on his answer phone, but Steve refused to return the calls feeling that Elton hadn't really supported him when the chips were down. Sometimes I acted the go between as one side would ask how the other side was and what they were up to.

Steve might have become something of a recluse refusing to take calls but his wife Gill was still talking to everyone and it was she who took me to a solo Elton John charity concert at The Queen Elizabeth Hall in London. If Steve was my surrogate dad, Gill was my surrogate mum. She had also grown up in the Salvation Army and, in a world that sometimes seemed to be full of madness, she was always an anchor of good sense. In a previous concert at the same venue a year earlier, Elton had been disturbed by Princess Margaret at the interval, when she walked into his dressing room only to find him in his underpants. The story had made all of the tabloid papers. Gill and I joked about this as we made our way backstage at half-time. True to form, when we entered the room, he was trouser less again. My mum had bought me a brand-new brown polyester suit for the concert but, as always, it was bought with plenty of room for me to grow into. I wanted to tell Elton how much I had enjoyed the concert, but all I can really remember about the chat, well apart from the underpants, was that he thought my suit was too big for me. (Many years later when I met Elton backstage prior to his concert at the Liberty Stadium in Swansea, Elton commented on how smart I was and what a great suit I was wearing. When I reminded him of his comments some 30 years earlier he couldn't believe he'd been so thoughtless and couldn't stop apologising.)

Gus was still incredibly busy with requests for him to produce artists other than Elton. He took his role as a record company director far more seriously than he had and he also started to produce some material by Kiki Dee. My career was on hold and Kiki's career had stalled a little as well, with all of the record company changes. It wasn't until Bias Boshell came up with a couple of songs including 'I've Got the Music in Me' that it started to get back on track. Bias, as you might remember, was the piano player David Costa had brought in for the original recording of 'I Don't Know How To Say Goodbye'. He had joined Kiki's band and they had all lived together in a big house, a bit like The Beatles in *Help!* Bias had played a couple of his songs to other members of the band who immediately recognised their commercial potential.

Clive Franks had started working on Kiki's follow-up album to *Loving and Free* but just like David Costa, he had been moved aside when Steve Brown left the company. Gus finished off the recordings and took the producer credit which became another massive feather in his cap when the song became a worldwide hit.

It's funny in life – but I believe there is a golden moment which can be lost very quickly. In many ways 1975 could well have been my golden moment but for a number of reasons beyond my control, that moment came and went. I was being produced by the top man in the world with the support of the most successful artist but, for one reason or another, the record wasn't being completed and time was moving on, for me, and the world of music. It's not surprising Gus wasn't available to finish off the tracks. As well as the success he was achieving with Kiki Dee, Elton had returned to the studio yet again and he needed a big hit because *Caribou* had been something of a critical failure. It had still topped the UK and Billboard charts for a number of weeks and the singles 'Don't Let the Sun Go Down on Me' and 'The Bitch is Back' where both top 20 singles, but there was a feeling that the next album had to be extra special.

I remember having dinner at Steve's home in Lenham when the album was being discussed. This album would be special to Elton because Bernie was writing their story. Up until this moment the songs had been Bernie's life but Elton would be 'Captain Fantastic' and Bernie would be the 'Brown Dirt Cowboy' and it confirmed to me that Bernie was a genius. The album charted their story from Tin Pan Alley hit-chasers to the early days of their success in the US. Of course as well as being Elton and Bernie's story, this was Steve's story too and, although he tried to maintain a disdainful distance, I'm sure he felt proud to see the way his contribution was acknowledged in the accompanying artwork.

That summer I spent a number of weeks staying at Steve's house and finally after a week or so of sharing the armbands with his pre-school children, I learnt to swim in his newly dug swimming pool. Without Steve at the heart of the record company, my career seemed to be drifting aimlessly. Gus was too busy and Steve wasn't talking to anyone directly on record except for the occasionally sarcastic letter or phone call to David Croker. Rocket appointed various new heads of A&R (Artists & Repertoire) who rarely stayed very long and so, I was starting to lose heart. It was suggested that another producer should be brought in to take over the project from Gus but although Gus was too busy to do the job, he didn't want to give the project up to anyone else.

By the time things became clearer at the record label, it was decided that releasing the first single from Gus's sessions would have to be held over until the New Year because it would get lost in the Christmas rush. Yet again I was devastated, it was hard to put my finger on it but I felt that my chance was slipping away. Gus had started the tracks some time earlier and in the meantime my voice continued to fall. Also, music was moving on and whereas my rock track 'When You're Away' had really excited me when first recorded, now it was starting to sound a little dated.

The autumn rolled on and back home one of the major changes was that our church started its own youth group meeting on a Friday. We had a lot of teenagers in the church and between them they took responsibility for the new venture. I was asked to sing most Fridays and that again encouraged me to write more songs as I had to keep coming up with new material.

The biggest consequence of that change at the church would eventually have more of an impact on my life than I could have imagined. In the west of Swansea was a small Gospel Hall, Castleton Chapel, Mumbles. Whereas we had lots of teenagers, they were quite a small group and they decided to join with us that autumn. One of that select group was a pretty young lady called Hilary, the daughter of the architect Philip Davies who had added the extension to my house. She was friendly, with one of the loudest laughs

I'd ever heard. The only problem I could see was that she was a dedicated Bay City Rollers fan. Like so many of the girls her age, she wore baggy jeans which were trimmed in tartan which she had sown on herself. She also had a tartan scarf but as the weeks went past I seemed to make more and more allowances for this 'Scottish weakness' although I would tease her as much as I dared when the chance presented itself.

Chapter 14

1976

The New Year started with snow and a walk with the church gang around the white byways of Gower. Hilary was my first choice for snowball target practice and I think the other kids were starting to talk. Things came to a head when I managed to cover her with a veritable avalanche as we passed underneath some trees.

It was early in January that another musical landmark occurred. Up until this point gospel music for me was either the Welsh hymn-singing I heard at Sunday teatime at my grandmother's house or the new, hip guitar groups like the Salvation Army-based band, the Joy Strings. To be honest, we bought tickets for a concert to be held at the Afan Lido in Port Talbot more out of duty than expectation. Not everyone wanted to go but I, together with my brother Gareth and Steven Payne from Mumbles, all decided we would give it a shot. I think Hilary only bought a ticket because I asked her if she wanted to come and she might have mistaken that as an offer of a date!

The concert featured Pat Boone singing with a Swedish Gospel choir and a second-half performance by an American band called Andraé Crouch & The Disciples. Pat Boone was fine, but to be honest we giggled through most of his performance as Steven Payne constantly called him Des O'Connor. And then for the second-half Andraé took to the stage with his band. There were loads of them including a brass section and a backing vocal group and when they started playing, I couldn't believe the sound. Most of the hymn-music I was used to was slow and in a minor key – this was just pure joy. Andraé was a short African-American who played the piano like Elton and sang like James Brown. The B3 Hammond organ screamed in the back over a groovy rhythm section. The songs were all about heaven but for me, this was a glimpse of heaven here on earth.

As soon as the concert finished I rushed to the back of the hall to buy an album. On the way back to Swansea I couldn't help but feel a little frostiness coming from the Bay City Roller fan. She thought I'd ignored her all the way through the second-half. What she didn't know was that I was completely lost in the music I had heard and the possibilities it might open up in my own music. Ignoring her, it never crossed my mind!

January moved soggily on but on Saturday the 24th January, my life was to change forever. I thought my friendship with Hilary was progressing quite well but it wasn't until I got a call from Kath Smith, one of the older teenagers in the church group, that I realised there was no turning back. Kath said Hilary had just rung her to say she was upset that I hadn't asked her out. She wasn't sure if I liked her as a friend or whether there might be more and she wanted to know. I put the phone down and thought for a minute before picking up the phone and dialling Hilary's home number.

The conversation went something like this:

"Hi, it's Maldwyn here."

"Oh hi," said Hilary.

"Kath said you wanted to ask me something."

"No! Kath said you wanted to ask me something," said Hilary.

"Right... will you go out with me?" I asked.

"Yes," she replied.

"Right," I said, "I'd better go."

"No," said Hilary, "Ask me again."

And with a simple telephone conversation started a relationship that has lasted 34 years! It was a week until I saw

Hilary at the youth club for what was a slightly awkward first meeting as boyfriend girlfriend, and the following day we all went to Brian Farr's house for his birthday party. Everyone was there, the Twins, Monty, Gareth, The Manley Brothers, Dai Veasey and of course my new girlfriend. Her dad came to pick her up and ever the gentleman, I escorted her to the door. I remember asking if she minded if I tied up her scarf. "No, I can do it," she said. Before she had had time to find it I had put it around her neck and pulled her towards me. Our first kiss, and although I'm not usually the type to kiss and tell I should say, it was the first of many!

Chapter 15

I'm sorry Gus doesn't work here anymore...

The year progressed on lots of fronts but in truth the music career seemed to be faltering. Gus was busy producing two Elton albums that year, *Rock of the Westies* and the double album *Blue Moves*. Elton himself also seemed a little distant or distracted whenever we met. It's well documented in other books that these years were difficult for Elton on a personal level and that lack of involvement from Elton led to a measure of drift at the record label. One by one, the original close team were leaving Elton and, without those voices trying to curb some of his more excessive tendencies, Elton's personal life seemed to become more unstable. This was the year that he sacked Dee Murray and Nigel Olsson from his band. They had been with Elton from the beginning and neither of them took it well. This was also the year that Elton finally came out. Today no one would bat an eyelid and to be honest nobody would have been surprised by Elton's announcement, but 1976 was a very different world. In those days I would almost come to blows with kids in school who would call Elton names but, with a declaration in one of the UK's national newspapers, there was no doubt left. For my parents and the culture they came from, these revelations where a major cause of concern and I'm sure it did make them question their decision to allow me to enter into that world.

The release of a single from the Gus Dudgeon sessions almost seemed like an afterthought. With the future still on Gus's mind, he decided to only use one track from the new sessions and included the song 'Hey Gunfighter' from the David Costa album with me double tracking the piano to cover the imperfections. The single was released with the B side giving the additional information 'before his voice broke'.

On a national level the single sank without trace. The world was moving on and even though I was only fifteen years old, I could tell the track sounded dated. The only good thing was that I made it into the charts of my local radio station. Independent radio stations were being granted broadcasting licenses and one of the first outside the main metropolitan areas was Swansea Sound. We were so excited as teenagers to have music broadcast in stereo that we even listened avidly to the test broadcasts. Every week the station would publish its own chart and 'When You're Away' peaked somewhere in the early teens, and to be honest the way things were going the same could be said of my career.

For me, there was the inconvenient distraction that this also was my O Level year. I was still surprised and disappointed that I was still in full-time education, as that had never been my plan, but as I was there I was expected to do the exams and also to try my best. In my mind this was all wrong, but I eventually got my head down for a week or so and managed to pass all of the exams without really excelling, but without embarrassing the family either.

In many ways the summer saved my sanity. 1976 was the summer of my teenage years – the long hot summer, the summer of drought and hose pipe bans. I spent those hot summer days either at camp down at Llanmadoc on the Gower with all of my friends from church or playing football and cricket down at Cwm Level Park. Hilary had to go away with her parents for a couple of weeks, but was back in time for Elton's concert at the Capitol Theatre in Cardiff. This was the first time I'd seen the new enlarged Elton John band which featured Roger Pope on drums and they were amazing.

Mum and dad, David the eldest, Gareth the middle one and me the baby. Manselton, Swansea 1963.

My first band! Mam on the piano and David on acoustic guitar. My dad, cousin Stanley and Uncle Colin and me at the front.

Always camera shy. Dressed as Ryan Davies' character from *Our House* in a fancy dress competition.

Swansea Schoolboys' football team: Welsh champions 1971. I'm third from the left in the middle row. The boy holding the ball is Jeremy Charles.

Performing my own song in front of the school in 1972.

With John Peel at my first Radio 1 session in July 1973.

Rocket Records promotion photograph.

Rocket promotion shot at Port Talbot steelworks.

What a body, sunbathing in Brynhyfryd!

The band that never was: friends Brian Farr, Phil Taylor and brother Gareth. I've still got the guitar, tartan cap and flares.

This photograph from the Gus Dudgeon sessions made the front page of the *Western Mail*. Always proud to be Welsh!

New haircut, new clothes – a teen idol!

Me aged 16 and Hilary aged 15 with friend Brian Farr on a Sunday school outing in Llanstephan.

Hil and me in Swansea Market's passport kiosk, 1979.

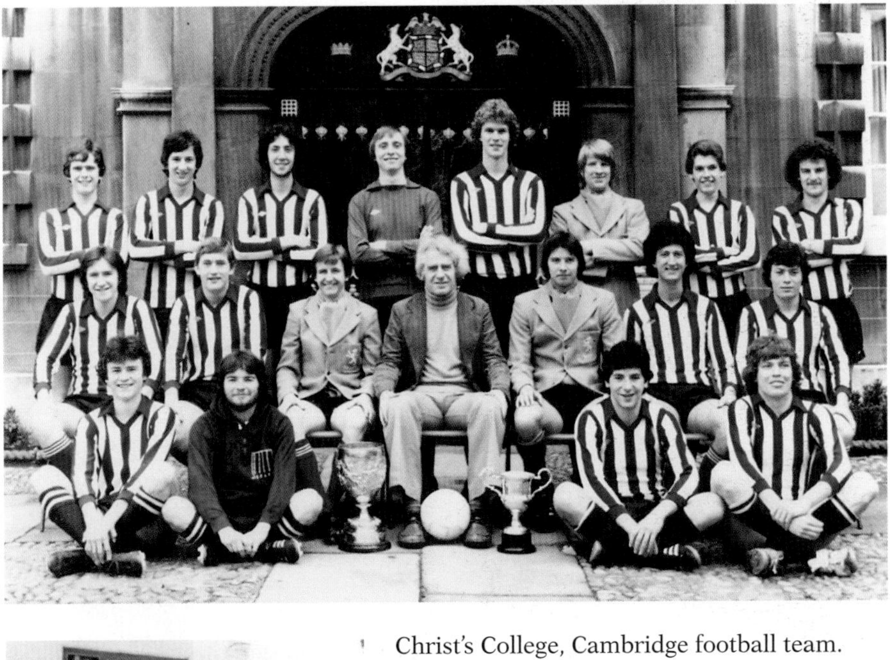

Christ's College, Cambridge football team. League and Cup winners.

Studying at Cambridge University for my finals.

Graduation day. Mum and dad, Mam and Hilary.

Hil and me on our engagement.

Always the bridesmaid...

...this time the bride!

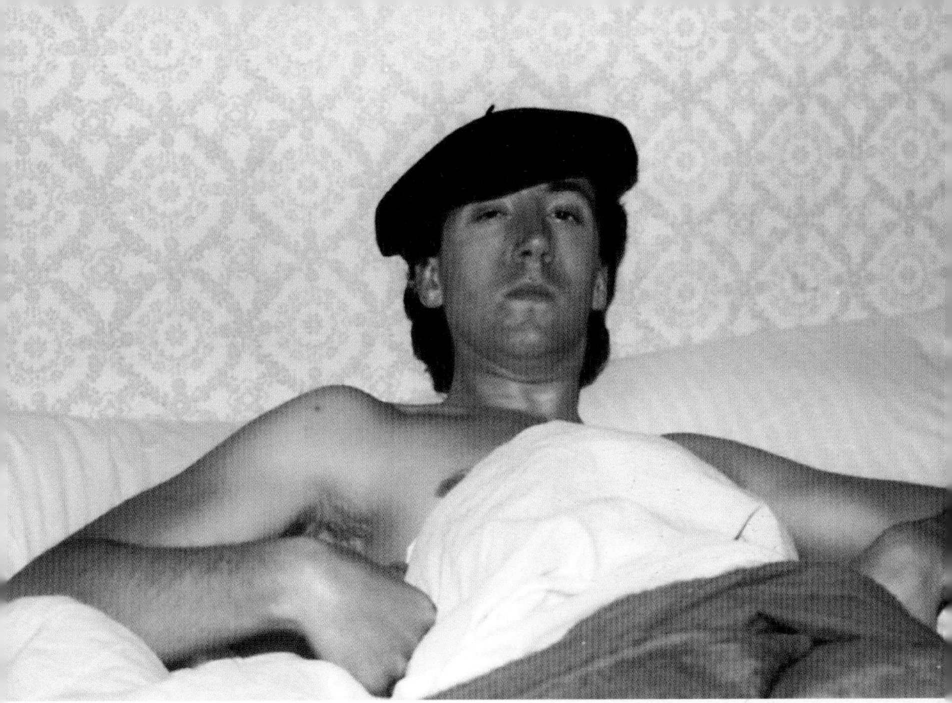

On honeymoon in France!

With my daughter Amy; she always was a studious girl.

With Amy and 'one-eyed' Jackson!

One of my favourite pictures of me and the kids.

HTV's new matinee idol!

With Max Boyce, the band and that leek on a beach in Australia.

Larry Page and Jade with Amy in the studio in Stoke-on-Trent.

Christmas dinner with After the Fire's Andy Piercy on our first writing weekend.

Rocking out on *The Mal Pope Show*.

On top of a New York skyscraper with Deborah Henson-Conant.

Driving around New York and standing up through the sunroof of a limousine with Downtown Julie Brown.

Christmas at the House of Commons with Neil Kinnock. Backing vocals from Rhodri Morgan, Ron Davies and Allan Rogers.

Backstage at the Royal Albert Hall with the Hollies.

Interviewing a one-time idol and now friend Ralph McTell.

With Catherine Zeta-Jones before we sang together on Radio Wales.

Picture from the *Sunday Mirror*. A concert at Brynhyfryd Primary School on the release of my first single.

After the concert, we met up with Paul Gambaccini. The last time I'd seen Paul was when he joined us on our Sunday school outing at Langland Bay on Easter Monday. Paul was as friendly as ever, and told us about the new Elton single. It was going to be a duet with Kiki Dee and Paul was convinced it would be massive. Fair play to Paul, he still knew his pop music and within a couple of weeks Elton found himself on top of the singles charts in the UK for the first time in his career.

Later, when I caught up with Gus he couldn't wait, as always, to share with me another one of his great stories. There was never any doubt that Kiki Dee was a great singer live, but it was always difficult to get that same energy on her recorded vocals. Elton and Bernie had written the duet with Kiki in mind and Gus had put together a really great pop backing track. In the studio, when it came time for Kiki to record her vocal, it just wasn't right. Nobody knew what to do except Elton. He went behind a recording screen, took off all of his clothes and when she tried a new take, he ran out and around the studio completely starkers. It definitely had the desired affect, as Gus said it was one of the best vocals he had ever heard from Kiki.

In many ways I had it all. Hilary and I both wore our matching 'Don't Go Breaking My Heart' T-shirts all summer long. I'd passed enough exams to keep everyone happy and my social life was nothing short of all consuming. As the nights started drawing in and everyone returned to school, life returned to normal fairly quickly.

When I had last spoken to Gus, the plan remained the same, that we would soon go back into the studio to complete the album. It was around this time that I got a call from David Croker at Rocket to let me know that Gus had decided to leave Rocket. There it was then, my second champion at the record company had left and I was now set adrift again. I did try to speak to Gus, but he was busy with the new studio he was building, and producing projects around the world, and we never really hooked up again. I think I took it fairly well initially, but over the weeks contact with the record company became less and less. What was I to do? I thought I'd try one last roll of the dice. Elton had moved from Virginia Water to an old Tudor mansion near Windsor. I found the address and sent him a letter. In it I said that I felt like a sixteen-year-old failure. I had lost my faith in music. Everyone who had believed in me at the record company had left and I didn't know what to do. I popped the letter in the post and carried on with my life. I knew Elton was busy travelling the world, so the chances of him receiving the letter personally were remote, but then again I had nothing else to lose.

As this was the school autumn term and I was at Dynevor School's Lower Sixth, there was plenty of time for other activities. Charles Dickens's *A Christmas Carol* had always been a favourite of mine, so when I was asked to audition for a part, I jumped at it. Cast as Scrooge's nephew, it was a fairly undemanding role but I really enjoyed the fun of being part of a theatrical production. The show finished at around 9.30 and I was more than happy to catch a bus back home. At the end of one performance, I walked to the bus stop to wait for a ride home when, driving pretty fast for my dad, I noticed him and my brother racing towards me. It was one of those moments where you are not sure what to worry about first. What family disaster could have brought them both out? "Quick" said Gareth. "Get in the car. Elton's been on the phone and he's calling back in half an hour."

When I got home I sat by the phone hoping that next door wouldn't tie up the line, as we shared a party line in those days, which meant if they were using the phone, we couldn't receive a call. Almost exactly to the moment he said he would call, the phone rang. It was Elton. He always called me Maldwyn as in Baldwyn rather than Maldwyn as in Malcolm and when he used my name in the conversation, I could tell he was serious. He said that I wasn't a sixteen-year-old failure and that he would be cross if I thought I was. He was now going to take control of my career and was going to produce my next record. He wanted me to get together all of my new songs and he would arrange a recording session to demo the songs early in the New Year. I came off the phone shell-shocked. I was also incredibly moved by Elton's actions. I think he could identify my feeling of failure with the emotions he had had as a struggling singer and he really wanted to make things right for me.

So here I was. Christmas was coming. I had my first girlfriend and Elton John wanted to produce my next record. The year 1976 hadn't turned out to be quite as bad a year as I thought it was going to be.

CHAPTER 16

Elton, Eric and Abbey Road Studios

I'D BEEN WORKING ON new songs using the tape recorder Gus had sent me and they were starting to mature. I was still drawing on inspiration for lots of different sources. Hilary was by now a fixture in my life and the life of my family, and it was one day, talking to her and her friend Adele that the lines 'If words were like the rain, I'd drown in your arms' came. A year or so earlier, they would have been too mushy for me but now, as a loved up sixteen-year-old, they were perfect additions to a song called 'If I Wasn't There'.

So, armed with half a dozen songs, together with my dad, I made the pilgrimage yet again to London to seek my fortune. I was worried because I was just getting over a cold, but I managed to lay down the tracks, some with my guitar and some with a grand piano. Elton seemed pleased with the results and he said we would soon be back into the studio to record them as masters.

Reading other accounts of Elton's life, it's obvious this was a difficult time for him, some claiming he was living as a semi-recluse. I think it's a testament to the man that he kept his word to a sixteen-year-old schoolboy from Wales. Having said that, it didn't happen very quickly; weeks turned into months before the sessions were finally arranged. I think Steve Brown also had something to do with getting the demos recorded as masters. At this stage Steve really was living as a recluse in his big house in Kent refusing to take calls from any of his previous business colleagues. I sent him a copy of the songs I had recorded and he replied to say he really liked them. He also said he had written to David Croker to say that they'd be mad not to record 'If I Wasn't There' as a single and if they didn't, it was likely that the 'great pop star in the sky' would make his ears fall off! Steve didn't have any actual power at Rocket, but I think his opinion still carried a lot of weight with those in the inner circle surrounding Elton.

David Croker was now in full charge at Rocket and, after careful consultation with John Reid who controlled Elton's diary, he had booked the sessions for the end of May. It was decided that I would go to London to meet Elton and the arranger, on the prior weekend which just happened to coincide with the FA Cup Final. As a director of Watford FC, Elton was always allocated tickets for the final. Knowing how much I loved football, Elton thought it would be a good idea if David and I went to the game and then went back to his house to meet the arranger. OK – this was the way I thought life was supposed to be, I really was back in the game!

David Croker met me at Paddington and we drove to Wembley. David was a keen West Ham supporter and had been in school with Trevor Brooking, so I don't think taking me to the final was any particular hardship. The old Wembley stadium was immense and the atmosphere electric especially as the finalists that year were old rivals Manchester United and Liverpool. Although Manchester United won 2–1; the goal I remember was a half volley from Jimmy Case which flew past Alex Stepney into the Manchester United goal right in front of David and me.

As soon as the match finished we jumped into David's car and headed off to Woodside. The house had apparently been built for the royal physician. It was close enough to Windsor Castle for the physician to be able to see a flag raised if his services were needed by the Royal Family. I had been impressed at the home in Virginia Water but this was something else. In many ways the house had yet to be fully 'Eltonised', but again it was easy to see he was still in a collecting phase. As I popped to the loo, I couldn't help but notice that carelessly leaning on the bottom step of the stairs was a lovely mahogany presentation case which contained a white dress. On a little plaque at the bottom of the case it noted that the dress had been worn by Judy Garland in *The Wizard of Oz*! For all of the classic memorabilia Elton had lying around the house, it seemed his most treasured possession when we arrived was a newly installed DJ set of turn tables. They were connected to a massive amplifier and speaker system and Elton insisted on playing a new track that he loved. He was dressed in a tracksuit and looked pretty relaxed. He ran to stand behind the decks and launched into The Tramps 'Disco Inferno'. It sounded immense and every time I hear or play that track now, I'm immediately transported back to that room at Elton's mansion.

Elton was doing a lot of concerts with Ray Cooper being the only other musician on stage. Ray was another rock 'n' roll character. He always looked immaculate, dressed in a jacket with a carnation buttonhole and had played percussion for everyone from the Rolling Stones to Pink Floyd. Elton seemed to place a lot of trust in Ray's judgement and it was Ray who suggested using a young arranger called Mike McNaughton who I think had been responsible for the music on the *Noddy* cartoon series.

We checked the keys again for the three songs we were going to record and then everyone left. Elton was his usual caring self, making toast with marmite and chatting in the kitchen about music. I told Elton that I'd really begun to like black gospel music and in particular Andraé Crouch who I'd seen at the Afan Lido. Elton had an incredible record collection which was stored in the house, all catalogued in alphabetical order. He jumped up and was gone for a couple of minutes only to return with an Andraé Crouch album and a couple of others by Aretha Franklin. It was a great night and maybe one of the only times when I spoke to him as a friend rather than being completely in awe of him being my idol. I told him about my new girlfriend and talked about school and especially football. That night I watched the FA Cup final again on a massive TV projector system and went to sleep in a gigantic four-poster bed marvelling at the extraordinary life I was living.

The following day, I headed back to Swansea and a weeks worth of school. Before leaving I met Elton's mum Sheila. She was pottering around in a little office set up in a corner of the mansion. She was lovely to me, asking about my school and family. One thing that struck me and has stayed with me ever since was a list on the wall. It listed all of Elton's cars and the dates when they had to be taxed and MOT'd. I'm not sure why that should have been such a surprise, because with so many cars I'm sure it was easy to lose track, but his mum was there to make sure he didn't forget the mundane jobs that even a superstar has to get right.

By Friday I was back to the smoke and off to the studio. I had worked in a lot of top class studios during my Rocket days but this took the biscuit. We were booked into Abbey Road. I got to the studio in the early afternoon and was ushered into the studio. Elton was already there as he'd been recording a charity single for a football charity called the Goaldiggers. I was always incredibly excited to see Elton but this room topped it all. Elton walked up to meet me and then he introduced me to his friends who had helped with the recording. The first famous face was Brian Moore, the TV football commentator. I had listened to him talk football most of my life and he was really friendly. Then Elton made one of the most unnecessary introductions I'd ever heard. "Maldwyn, this is Eric Morecambe."

In 1977, on a list of British celebrities, Eric Morecambe even trumped Elton John. Eric was fantastic. He asked me where I was from and I said Swansea. "Swansea – that was where Ernie and I did our first gig." Before the war

Ernie Wise had been a successful member of impresario Jack Hylton's stable. Ernie had seen Eric audition for Jack Hylton in Manchester and had been very impressed, but war meant a lot of the theatres closed down and Eric was never given the opportunity to join the travelling entertainment troupe. In post war 1946 Britain, there was a need for entertainment and the provincial theatres started to take touring productions once again. Ernie was invited by Jack to perform at the Swansea Empire in a show called *Youth Takes A Bow*. Eric Bartholomew was also invited to be part of the show and, together with his mother Sadie, he made the trip south from his home in Morecambe, the place that would give him a new stage name. Eric and Ernie met in Swansea and it was on the Empire stage that they performed together for the very first time.

The other thing that struck me was what a gentleman Brian Moore, the football commentator, was and how he seemed interested in listening to me talk about Swansea City as much and more than he liked hearing his own voice. This was in stark contrast to the distinctly cold greeting I had experienced at the BBC Club following a John Peel session. We had completed the recording and I was waiting to be picked up by Steve Brown. So, we were waiting in the BBC Club with John Walters. I was young and there were a couple of long-haired music types there, but I got the dirtiest of looks from a number of very well-known football and sports presenters who were hanging onto the bar. They were talking just loud enough for us to hear them complain that, as a kid, I shouldn't be in their bar. I think that when John Walters returned the compliment with a couple of colourful four-lettered descriptive words, they put their glasses on the bar and left!

Eric Morecambe was as football mad as Brian Moore, Elton and me. He was a director of Luton FC and with football as our common denominator, the middle-aged comedian, the rock star, the TV football commentator and the teenage kid from Wales talked for a good half-an-hour before Eric and Brian left. We had an hour or so to wait until the studio was ready to start the session. As always, Elton was great company but I thought he was looking a little rough around the edges. His hair was long and quite scraggy and I thought his eyes looked tired and quite sad.

This session was very different to the way I had worked before. There was no sitting around listening to the song and everyone making it up as we went along. This time, the arranger had taken my piano parts and written a full arrangement to support my song from drums and bass to full orchestra. The orchestra would be added later so I didn't have to play with them, but to be honest I had more than enough on my plate with the rhythm section. As I couldn't read music, the only one without a score in front of them was me. As well as Elton, I also knew the engineer on the session, Clive Franks. Clive was the man responsible for Elton's live sound and also the engineer Elton used on a number of studio projects including the first Kiki Dee album. Clive was an old friend of people like Stuart Epps, and could always be relied upon to give Elton an honest opinion, and in a sea of new people, he was another friendly face.

In fact everyone was going out of their way to make me feel comfortable and put me at ease. I'm sorry to say that I didn't down write down the name of the musicians, although I think the guitarist had the nickname 'Froggy'. The rest of the studio band comprised a bass player (who doubled on double bass) and a drummer, whilst the percussion was played by Elton's right-hand man of the time, Ray Cooper. I'm not sure whether it was because Elton was the producer and was listening to me play or whether it was because I was in Abbey Road with a studio full of musicians who all had music in front of them or whether it was because I was growing older and was losing the courage of childhood – but for the first time in a recording studio I was feeling nervous.

Mike McNaughton, the arranger, actually conducted the band (including me) making sure the tempo set was spot-on to work with his string ideas. With all of this going on it's no wonder that I was having a bit of trouble. Years later, John Reid sent me the 24-track tapes for me to remix and add my mature voice to and at one stage Elton can be heard saying to me that I was speeding up a little and I needed to relax into the track.

There was one thing no one had thought of. The track needed a guide vocal so that everyone could be sure that we were in the right places and that the arrangement was working. I was playing the piano, and if I sang as well, there would be "spill" on the piano mikes. Also, I needed to concentrate on getting the piano parts right. There was no alternative – Elton would have to leave his producer's chair in the control room and sing guide vocals. So let's think about this, I'm sixteen years old and at Abbey Road studios surrounded by top session musicians, all reading music and playing songs that I had written and Elton John is singing my song. It's not surprising I was a little tense is it? We had three songs to record and eventually we got takes that Elton, Clive and Mike McNaughton were happy with. And with that, I went back to Elton's house and collapsed into bed exhausted.

The following day I went back into Abbey Road to record my vocals. They went down quite quickly and then came the time to do the backing vocals. I had a couple of attempts but it sounded like me answering myself. It was at this moment that all of my prayers were answered. Elton turned to Clive and said "Shall I have a go?" And there it was, Elton John was singing backing vocals on my tracks and they would be there forever!

The only other thing we had to do was record the strings. I'd never been to a string session before and found it fascinating. The strings were organised by a London session fixer, who had at his disposal some of the finest orchestral players in the world. These players probably earned more money from these pop sessions than they did in their proper classic jobs, but although they loved the money, they weren't always terribly interested in the job until the red light went on. Elton had told me what would happen and Clive made sure we listened in to the various conversations going on in between takes. Most of the players would have newspapers in their hands or would be chatting about the football until the very last moment, when the red light went on and Mike McNaughton raised his baton. Then they became the seasoned musicians and were playing the arrangement notes perfectly. The red light went off and straight away they returned to the newspaper crossword puzzles and the conversations that had been so rudely interrupted by the recording.

It is still very hard to put into words the feeling that a big string section creates and that feeling is multiplied a thousand fold when the music they are playing is yours. Today, synthesizers and sampling machines can create a very good reproduction of an orchestra, but in reality, there is no comparison. It's the imperfection, the slight human timing difference between the violins and cellos. It's organic and totally overwhelming. I am emotional, I always have been, and hearing the strings for the first time brought me to tears.

Elton turned to me during the session and saw I looked upset. He wanted to know what was wrong and I had to cough a little, pull myself together and say, "Elton I'm just so happy!" And I really was. Elton and Clive Franks made sure I had a rough mix to take home to play to Hilary and my friends and so, I headed for Paddington and home. The next time I saw Elton was at the SARM West Studios where he was mixing my tracks. It was typical that when a director left Rocket, and one of the other directors that were left on the board said that they would take responsibility for the company, they didn't do it in half measures. When Steve left

Gus, he started producing everyone on the roster and when Gus left Elton, he did the same, producing me, Kiki Dee and another new Scottish band called Blue! (No, not that one.)

The last time we met up was at Watford. It must have been around the time that Graham Taylor had taken over as the new manager. I'd gone to a game and then been invited back to the clubhouse afterwards for a drink. Elton was there, together with some of his close family. I spent most of the evening in the company of one of his female cousins. She was really sweet to me and she told me how much Elton thought of me and that he really was a special caring person. As the night drew to a close, I was heading back to my hotel in London and Elton was driving back to Windsor. Before leaving he took me aside and said how much he was enjoying the recording. He then said, "If there's anything you ever need to talk to anyone about and you can't find anyone at home to listen to you, you have to know you can always phone me. You've got my number. I'll always be there." With that, he was gone and I was heading back to Wales.

It's very strange to think but that evening probably marked the highest point in my friendship with Elton and the highest point in my position at the record company. In reality, with the clarity of hindsight, it also marked the end of my career at Rocket.

CHAPTER 17

'If I wasn't there...'

ELTON'S TELEPHONE NUMBER NEVER stayed the same for long. It had to be constantly changed because one way or another fans seemed to be able to get hold of it and then they'd ring him for a chat. It would be another five or six years until I would see him again.

It's not as if we mixed in the same social circles. His life was becoming more and more complicated and he seemed to spend more of his time in the US than he did in Britain. I was back in Wales, waiting to hear how we were going to promote the new single 'If I Wasn't There' which featured Elton on backing vocals. One of the problems was that I wasn't a priority. My name would be advertised in the big US music paper *Billboard* magazine along the other Rocket stable-mates like Cliff Richard and Kiki Dee, but I was only making up the numbers. What I found out was that people were only really interested in me while Elton was interested. Pete Brown, Steve Brown's brother was working for John Reid's management company as the personal manger for Queen. (My mum was ever so impressed with this until I clarified the position saying they were a rock royalty not actual royalty! She was never really one to be completely up on pop music. For the first eighteen months of my career with Rocket, she would insist on calling him John Elton rather than the other way around.) He told Steve that when Elton had finished the tapes John Reid, sent an urgent telex from the US asking the office to dig up my management contract. I'd never signed one, so, I could still have Steve as my representative. Having said that, he still wouldn't speak to anyone and if your manager won't speak to your record company, it probably wouldn't do your long-term career prospects much good.

Another problem was that one of the other artists Elton was producing for Rocket at the time, Blue, were starting to become successful. I saw with my own eyes that their manager was in the Rocket office at every opportunity, badgering and cajoling the staff to work on his boys, and that persistence and tenacity was reaping benefits. Blue were flown to New York to launch their album, performing at a club with Elton and Kiki and later at a party that had guests including Paul Simon and Shirley Maclaine.

My single launch was a little, shall we say, low key. This wasn't for lack of effort on the part of the new PR lady at Rocket, Laura Beggs. Laura, together with David Croker, was one of the only people I felt I could trust at the label. When it came to fashion, I wasn't particularly trendy, just your average Swansea teenager in flared jeans and a T-shirt. She organised a make over for the release of the single. I was taken to a warehouse in Covent Garden, where a number of trendy outfits were selected for me and then I was taken for my new haircut. When I finally looked in the mirror at the blow-dry construction on my head, I hardly recognised myself. At last I looked a little like the other teen idols who had been successful over the past few years. The trouble was, just as I was getting the teeny bop treatment, the world of music was changing very fast, faster than the record companies knew. In 1977, the Sex Pistols were sacked by EMI records for swearing on TV. In 1977, I was releasing 'If I Wasn't There', a romantic ballad with lush strings and Elton John on backing vocals, looking a bit of a ponce! If my timing wasn't great in the studio, it was catastrophic in career terms.

At least there was some interest from the media in Wales and Laura came down to Swansea for a couple of days to help co-ordinate a concerted Welsh media campaign. The most important element was filming a video for the BBC's early-evening news programme *Wales Today*. Hilary would have been the obvious candidate to play opposite me as my romantic partner, as she had been the inspiration for the song, but unfortunately she was in school that afternoon and I think her parents, coming from the same church culture that I came from, weren't too keen on her appearing on television. In the end Laura had to act as stand-in, walking arm in arm with me through Clyne Park.

Apart from getting recognised a little more regularly in Swansea, the record sank without trace. Over the coming months, new faces came into the record company in the A&R department and with them came new signings and new priorities. Having played my Elton trump card, I had no more cards to play. In reality, I knew it was over but it would be a couple of years before I would officially leave Rocket, but in the meantime there was my education to think about.

Having parents who were teachers meant that no matter what was happening in my music life, my education was still a priority for them. The new school year dawned with no hit record and with the pressure starting to mount in my A Level year. I was studying three subjects: mathematics, computer science and economics. Something strange was beginning to happen. I was starting to enjoy studying economics! The 1970s were a time of great changes in Britain. The oil crisis, the winter of discontent, three-day weeks, IMF loans and North Sea oil discoveries. Coal strikes, power cuts and doing my homework and song writing in candlelight had been a regular part of my teenage years. More than once, I had been delayed at Paddington or stopped from walking down a London street because of the bomb threats of the IRA. I had always had a great interest in the news, dating I think from my last year of primary school, when every day Mr Morlais Williams would set a news quiz. We would be expected to watch the news every night and the following day arrive in school with ten questions based on what we had seen. He would choose ten questions from those supplied. My mark for the year was 100 per cent and in the meantime I had become a news junkie! As I entered my final school year, my fascination with world events was being reflected in my economics class and I couldn't help myself. I was enjoying it.

By this time my brother David had graduated from Cambridge and it became apparent that my mum and dad thought I should follow in his footsteps. My school seemed to agree and I applied to Christ's College, the same college that David had been to. I was invited for an interview and travelled there on my own, staying overnight. The interview started with the Director of Studies looking down at a sheet of paper. "You're brother was here?" "Yes" I replied, "he really enjoyed himself here." Without looking up he said "He got a 2.2 didn't he... so you've nothing to live up to!" Well that's that I thought but whether it was a particularly bad year or whether he had decided that I was going to be the token Welsh comprehensive school candidate, a few weeks later a letter arrived offering me a place at the college so long as I got three A grades at A Level. No pressure then!

The year passed without many interruptions from London. Steve Brown sold his house and bought a farm and retired form the music business. For the first time, I really was on my own. I got my head down and concentrated on my studies. I did take the role of Pharaoh in a school production of *Joseph and the Amazing Technicolor Dreamcoat*, a production which also featured a fellow member of the school Christian Union, Kevin Johns, which was a welcome distraction but as the summer approached the pressure grew.

Chapter 18

It's Cambridge for me

I FOUND IT HARD to sleep the night before getting my A Level results and woke early to get ready to go to the school to see how I had got on. I didn't have to wait too long as Mr Bernard Norris had got into school early, checked the results and rung us at home to congratulate me on getting into Cambridge. My grandmother had popped to the shops early that morning and when I greeted her at the bottom of the garden with "It's Cambridge for me," all she could say was, "I do hope so!" When I said the headmaster had rung to say I was in, she dropped her shopping and gave me the biggest hug I'd ever had. I'm sure she was hugging me for herself and also for her husband George who never got the chance to complete his education.

Although I knew I was privileged to get the university place, my head was still in the music. With Steve becoming a shepherd and training sheepdogs in Kent, I thought it would be best to speak to John Reid. Within a week of getting the results I went to London to talk about my future at Rocket, with the full intention of dumping university if I got the slightest encouragement from John. The initial deal was coming to an end but John said they were still committed to me as an artist and that he and Elton were very proud of my achievement. They thought the opportunity was too good to miss. I could continue to write and mature at university and they would come up to visit me as well. I suddenly had a vision of Rolls Royce cars and hamburgers. I left London with the realisation that my education was going to continue for another three years.

Christ's College was great fun, but I quickly realised when I got there, and this might sound a little odd, that I wasn't academic. I did buy two books whilst in Cambridge. One was a second-hand book on economics; the second was a boxed set of C S Lewis's *Narnia* series. Students were divided into various groups. There were toffs, swots and hearties. Well I definitely wasn't posh; I certainly wasn't a swot but there was a chance I could be hearty. The first thing that struck me when I got there was the quality of the football pitches. I'd played on some good grounds back home but these were like bowling greens, with nets and a clubhouse where we entertained our opponents after each game. And boy did we train. I had gotten quite soft since my footballing peak and it came as quite a shock with the new training regime. By the time I ran out to play my first game, I was physically exhausted. My life in college was to centre on the football team and the Christian Union. Hilary would often pop up to Cambridge for the weekend which always ended in tearful farewells at Cambridge station on Sunday nights.

Two things strike me, looking back. Firstly, I spent a lot of the time at university scared and secondly, my head was usually somewhere else, either back in Swansea or in London thinking about the music. You might have thought that after all of my trips to London, meeting some of the world's biggest music stars, that I would have been full of self-confidence but I wasn't. I always felt not quite good enough, compared to my fellow students. In London I had always been the kid invited into a strange new world. Here I was with my contemporaries, and this was supposed to be my world now as well.

The first night in my little room I woke to find my next-door neighbour had invited me to a 'Sherry – At Home' in his little room the following day. Richard Harden later went on to found *Harden's UK Restaurant Guide* but even then, he enjoyed the finer things in life. It took me some time to see past his blazers and bow ties and I'm sure he must have found his long-haired Welsh jeans-wearing musician neighbour a disappointment, but over the coming weeks we became good friends. And that maybe sums the situation up. People appeared so confident and self-assured and I didn't. I think a lot of it could be put down to their public school upbringing but, then again, all of my contemporaries had been high-flyers in their old lives and many brought that self-belief with them. It was only later that they let their guards down and I put aside my own fears and realised that we had the same worries and concerns and a lot more in common than I thought.

With regards wanting to be somewhere else, my problem was that my life in Swansea was very good; a group of great friends who did everything together and a girlfriend still at school. Every phone call or letter from home just reminded me that I was missing out. The other thing that wouldn't let me go was my music. Things were quiet with Rocket, so I decided to write to Jeff Griffen, a producer at BBC Radio 1. He had always been very supportive and he wrote back offering a session for the Andy Peebles show which was booked for the following spring.

The Christmas term came and went by in a flash, marked by Christ's College winning the Intercollegiate League at football. Coming from my chapel background I found some of the college names difficult to use in their new context. For example our big football rivals were Jesus College. No one ever used the 'college' part of the title so, when one of the games turned a bit tasty, the college magazine had a headline along the lines of 'Christ's play Jesus – All Hell Breaks Loose'. I must admit I found it difficult, to say the least.

The longer the spring term progressed, the less I found myself interested in my economics course. The college football success continued in the cup competition, spurred on by the inspirational leadership of an Irishman called Micky McGuire. The football club had a collective name of the 'footie monster' as we all met at Micky McGuire's room before going to dinner. The team knew I wrote songs and I offered to write an anthem for us to sing prior to every cup match. As we won each round, I would write a new verse to celebrate and inspire us to even greater heights next time. It seemed to work as we coasted to victory in the final. It was around this time in Cambridge that I changed my name; well I didn't change it, I had it changed for me. Maldwyn had always been a problem for people across Offa's Dyke but in Cambridge, I lost it for good. The football team was full of nicknames, The Thont, Winker Watson, Micky Cully. Maldwyn was too much of a mouthful for anybody, so I became Mal.

I had new batch of songs written and ready for the Radio 1 session. It was scheduled to be played out during my Easter holiday, one song every night. The week of transmission coincided with our college tour of Dublin which had been arranged by John Robbie, a graduate member of our soccer team, who was also an Irish rugby international. Every night I would tune in a little transistor radio hoping to catch the session. A couple of days into the week and during a phone call home, I was told that James Rubinstein from the A&R department at CBS had sent a telegram asking me to get in touch. The next day I rang him and arranged to go to London to meet him on my way back to Cambridge. I was still a Rocket man at heart but the enthusiasm from a new label seemed too good to turn down. Muff Winwood was head of A&R and he had been friends with Elton for many years. Maybe it was because he already knew all about me and felt I wasn't new at all or maybe the other songs on the session during the week weren't good, but by the time I met James, the fire seemed to have cooled and that door was closed.

I was still in contact with Rocket and it was around this time I got a letter from David Croker asking if I could help with arranging a concert for a new Rocket artist called Judy

Tzuke. I contacted the Cambridge Union and explained the situation. They weren't interested in promoting the concert but they would allow me to hire the main chamber. I did everything I could to get an audience, covering the whole of Cambridge in Judy Tzuke posters, even offering a free single on the door. The band arrived with an articulated truck full of gear which filled the chamber. This was not a bad thing because we didn't fill the chamber with an audience. In fact, most of those who did come were members of my college football team. Judy spent the whole evening singing to her drummer before the guitarist in her band implored her to speak to the audience. All she could say was "I don't know what to say, I've never done this before!" Earlier this year I interviewed Judy on the release on a new CD which contained songs from those Rocket years. Judy told the story about how she got her record deal, a story she has told many times over the years. She had heard about Rocket Records signing a young kid after hearing his session on the radio. Encouraged by that story, she had sent in a cassette of her songs to the label and they had signed her too. She was most surprised that after all this time, I was able to round off her story by telling her that I was the kid that Rocket signed.

I returned to Cambridge for the full Easter term and my exams. After two terms of lectures and supervisions, in truth, I was still relying on my A Level knowledge to get me through. I decided that it was time to change and started looking at various options. Anglo-Saxon Norse and Celtic looked good, as did Criminology. The subject that really caught my eye was Theology. I was working on the assumption that with a lifetime of Bible study under my belt already, how hard could it be? I mentioned the idea to my Director of Studies and he arranged for me to meet a Fellow of Christ's who also happened to be an old boy from my school in Swansea.

I met the young Fellow at Westcott House where he had his rooms. He invited me in and made a nice pot of tea which he served together with a big plate of biscuits. He looked like a proper 'holy man' reminding me of some vague image I held in my head of Rasputin. For about half an hour he allowed me to talk, to tell him my history, my need to change subjects and why I thought I would enjoy Theology. When I finally ran out of words, the room went silent for a moment. He slowly lowered his head looked over his glasses and through a set of big bushy eyes he held my gaze. "Mal," he said, "It's not for you". Dr Rowan Williams was already gaining for himself a reputation as being one of the leading theological minds of his generation, something that had already set him apart and marked him out as a potential future Archbishop of Canterbury, but it was obvious, even then, he was also a good judge of character. He saw through me straight away and I think he feared that my simple faith might not survive the battering such a degree would ensure and that with my commitments to football and music, the dedication I would need to study Greek and Hebrew was also in grave doubt. Over the years Rowan has been an incredible support for any number of projects I have been involved with on TV and the stage. There is only one thing that makes me cross when I think of Rowan. He has a brain full of great thoughts which I would love to hear, but every time I meet him he has a way of working that let's me do all of the talking. The time passes and I've unburdened myself about something or another and he's hardly said a word. We say goodbye and then I realise, he's done it again! Next time I swear, I'll be quiet and listen… next time!

CHAPTER 19

How I missed *Chariots of Fire*

AS WELL AS WRITING to Jeff Griffen at Radio 1, that Easter term I wrote to BBC Radio Wales. Megan Emery had been a researcher at *Wales Today* when my last Rocket single had been released. So I decided to write to her saying that I was going to be home for the summer and would it be possible to visit the station to see how programmes were made. The morning show *AM* was presented by a young journalist and musician called Chris Stuart and for two weeks I travelled back and forth to Llandaff in Cardiff. It wasn't long before I was put to work and the first proper 'research' job was to write a brief about the Welsh actor and writer Emlyn Williams. I read his autobiography and put together a list of questions and expected answers for Chris to use. I was surprised and delighted that, come the day of the interview, he followed the line of questioning I suggested and also thanked me at the end of the interview for doing a good job. And so began a relationship with BBC Radio Wales, that started as a summer job in 1979 as a researcher, and which over the coming thirty years would take me through every department ending up as a regular presenter. But that was some way off.

That summer was also memorable for another reason. Hilary had done well in her A Levels and had been accepted for teacher training in Bristol. I wasn't worried that the relationship wouldn't survive the distance, as we'd already had a year separated by the breadth of the United Kingdom. But I thought that with a university full of young men about to come her way, it was probably best to stake my claim properly. Armed with the money from the Andy Peebles show session, we bought a ring and became engaged on Hilary's eighteenth birthday.

My second year at Cambridge followed a very similar path. I had decided to join the Land Economy department, a small and exclusive group of students made up of true hearties (I shared lectures with a number of England international rugby players) some toffs (one of my supervision partner's father owned Argyllshire!) and a couple of swots who wanted to follow the career path of becoming a Chartered Surveyor. All I wanted to do was play, and I didn't mind if it was football or music. As well as being a stalwart of the college team, I started playing for the university second-IX, which was seen as a stepping stone to joining the Blues squad. As a part-time member of the Eagles, I had a number of eye-opening trips to play against public schools like Charterhouse. I was performing more and more regularly in some of the folk clubs, encouraged by a number of active club secretaries and had become something of name at those events, usually headlining a gathering in some college bar or other.

I was starting to get used to the very different life experiences the college offered. There was a cafeteria where we often eat as a football team, but on special occasions or when we were playing hosts to family and friends, we would put on our academic gowns and take dinner in Lower Hall. The food was the same, but the eating in the candlelit Dining Hall which dated back to the sixteenth century was always special. One of the regular highlights was when one of the scholars, charged with reciting the college 'grace' prior to dinner, would attempt to break the grace speed record. Everyone knew what was happening but the Fellows and Master would always look as if the garbled grace was a usual event… which it probably was and had been for hundreds of years.

It was during this time that I was invited to return to Cambridge a week early to be a part of film which was looking for authentic Cambridge University student extras. The people making the film had good credentials. David Puttnam had a good reputation as a producer and I remembered Colin Welland from the TV series *Z Cars* but the film synopsis didn't sound too good to me. A film about two runners from the 1920s, one a missionary the other a student, didn't bode well to me and anyway, why would I want to leave Swansea a week early and miss out on all the fun at home. And so it was I turned down the opportunity to be in *Chariots of Fire*. Every time I watch the film, I still see the faces of the boys I used to study with.

Things had also started to change at Rocket with the arrival of a new man in charge of publishing. I was invited down to London to meet with him and a record producer named Mark London. Eric Hall was a small man who more than made up for his lack of size by having the biggest personality I'd ever encountered. He'd been an actor, singer and as a promotions man, he'd arranged for the Sex Pistols to appear on TV! Eric was just over five feet and sported a Kevin Keegan curly perm. He always had a big cigar in his hand and he had a slight lisp which made his catch phrase "Monster Monster" even more memorable. I had a letter from Eric saying he had been through the Rocket back-catalogue and that he really liked my songs. As a publisher, he wanted to work with them and he also wanted to look at putting me back in the studio.

Every time I met Eric I kept thinking he shouldn't be a human, he should be a cartoon. His Jewish heritage shone through when he called me and everyone else 'Bubula' (a Yiddish term grandmothers use for children), and I loved him. After a lot of insipid people had sat in that chair, at last, here was a real character. For all of Eric's eccentricities, when it came to music, Mark London was the real deal. He'd written 'To Sir With Love' for Lulu, along with a lot of her other hits and he knew how songs worked. He had also been through my back-catalogue and found a number of tunes he thought were good but not finished and, possibly for the first time in my life, I had a lesson in song writing from a real craftsman. One song in particular I had recorded twice already, but he said it didn't get to the right place, it was missing the middle eight. We sat at the piano and he encouraged me to find the missing piece and within ten minutes I had, he said the song was now finished. I also recorded a couple of new songs which Mark said he was impressed with. Armed with those demos, Eric went to John Reid to put together a budget to record some new masters.

Some weeks passed before the sessions were booked at Air Studios on Oxford Street. The first session laid down the rhythm section and vocals and the following weekend, I returned to London with Hilary to hear the string section being recorded. One thing for sure, they really didn't cut any corners. We recorded three tracks with a view to finding a single. For all of Mark's encouragement and all of Eric's bluster and "Monster Monster", Rocket couldn't be persuaded to release another record. The tracks were farmed around for a while, picking up a cover by one of the Nolan sisters but as far as Rocket was concerned that was that.

The summer was spent travelling up and down the M4 as I supplemented my student grant by researching for Radio Wales. With a year to go as a student and a commitment made to Hilary, I really had to start making plans. The boss at the *AM* programme was a former journalist named David Nicholas. He had a crusty exterior which could frighten at times, but a wealth of experience and local knowledge that could fill a programme with guests and items with the least amount of effort. Before returning to Cambridge for my final year, David called me into his office. David wasn't one to hand out compliments for their own sake but he told me that he thought I had promise and that come the end of my time at university, he'd like me to join his team. I told David that I was still sure that I was going to London to concentrate on my music, but could I keep in touch. He agreed, we shook hands and I left for my final year as a student.

Chapter 20

The end of my academic career

It was some time during my last year at Cambridge that a letter dropped into my college pigeonhole from Pete Brown. Pete was Steve Brown's younger brother and for a number of years he had been the personal manger for Queen on behalf of John Reid. As personal manager he was on call twenty-four hours a day, sorting out any and all problems that might arise for your average rock band which included Freddie Mercury. As a John Reid employee, the salary was good but Pete now felt that, with his experience and contacts, it was time to strike out on his own. Pete had decided to set up his own management company in association with the rock promoter Harvey Goldsmith and they would like to chat to me about taking over my management contract.

When I met Pete in London, he still didn't have an office but he did have a lot of confidence and front, and he was convinced that he could make things happen for me. The first thing he did was organise a meeting with Rocket. We went in and shook hands. Pete spoke for ten minutes saying that Rocket hadn't lived up to its obligations and that he was taking me from them. The guy who held the Rocket hot seat at the time didn't get a word in and I left feeling very impressed. Then I went to meet Harvey Goldsmith. Harvey was just the business. He talked the business; an air of power surrounded him and people jumped when he barked out his orders. I was joining a management roster which was quite small and select, but it did include Van Morrison and Billy Connolly!

The Harvey connection suddenly opened a whole new

world of concerts and VIP tickets. All I had to do was ring the office and they'd put my name on the list. In a couple of weeks I saw Eric Clapton, the Average White Band and Bruce Springsteen, all from the best seats in the house.

Although Pete and Harvey were successful, they weren't keen on spending their own money if at all possible. We needed a company to start funding the new project and, with the song writing still flowing, the first thing Pete and Harvey organised was a new publishing deal with Terry Slater at EMI Publishing. (Terry would go on to become the manager of a-ha.) I might have looked forward to seeing some cash go towards an uncertain future, but after a lot of nagging, I managed to get them to pay for a new Gibson 355 guitar and a Vox AC30 amplifier. Well, at least I could sell them if it didn't work out.

Throughout this time I was talking to Pete about a new band called After the Fire who came from the same church background as I did. I don't think I was a particularly big Bible basher at this time, but Pete definitely had a problem with church, having rebelled against his Salvation Army background at around the same time as his brother Steve. I finally got Pete to listen to some After the Fire which he described as just another pop band. Well, at least I tried.

I had also started working with some young musicians in Swansea. I'd known Tony Kiley since my early school days and he'd always been the drummer in school productions. Andrew 'Wal' Coughlan had a fearsome reputation; he was a mean bass player with an ambition to go to London. We started rehearsing in Tony's back bedroom and were occasionally joined by a wizard keyboard player Nigel Hopkins, who the boys played with in another band whilst I was in university. As the months passed, Tony's parents wanted some peace and quiet in their lives, so we decided to cover my dad's garage in offcuts of carpets and became a real 'garage band'. I had recently discovered Bruce Springsteen. Our college cinema club couldn't actually charge entry to see the films so everyone had to by a raffle ticket before the film would start. One week, I won a record token and spent it on the Bruce Springsteen boxed set. Hearing the epic six-minute songs telling the stories of life on the New Jersey seaboard, I was encouraged to do the same for Swansea and, with the boys' encouragement, we started to create something unique.

As I came to the end of my time at university, I started to look back at the people I'd met. During my time, Billy Graham the evangelist had held a mission for the students. The first meeting was a disappointment as, it seemed to me, he was too aware of his audience, he was trying to speak from his head and trying to come up with an intellectual argument for finding faith, a bit like St Paul when he went to Athens for the first time. Someone must have had a word with him because, for the rest of the week, he spoke more from his heart and suddenly he made sense, his words had a real power and a lot of people found themselves with a lot to think about.

Another encounter which left a lasting impression on me was with the music impresario Jonathan King. At this time King was at the height of his showbiz power, with music business interests and also presenting a number of TV and radio shows. The venue was the Cambridge Union. Jonathan King and Paul Gambaccini had been invited to talk about the music industry and then take questions from the audience. Because I had a record deal and was performing all over the university, I was asked also to address the Union and then contribute to the discussion. With King and Gambaccini in the room (two Radio 1 stalwarts at the time), it was not surprising that no one really wanted to ask me any questions. At the end of the evening, I turned to King and said that they hadn't really needed me to be there. He turned and looked me straight in the eye and through that crooked smirk that became his trade mark feature he said, "No, we needed the amateur touch!" Nice guy!

My final year in college saw me sharing a double room with my best friend Paul Cassidy, a conscientious working-class lad from Newcastle, who shared my faith and love of football. I nearly got us both fined when I managed to spell out the words Swansea City, one letter at a time on our windows which overlooked Second Court and the Masters Lodge (when Swansea City were promoted to the football First Division). It was a great three years, but I was more than ready to get on with the rest of my life. And so my university career came to an end. I got my degree, a 2:2. So nothing to live up to for anyone following on from me either.

Chapter 21

'The streets of London'

If I was going to live in London, I would need a place to stay. Hilary had a cousin living in Wealdstone, north London, so I gave him a call and asked if he needed a roommate. The guy sharing his flat was moving out at the end of the summer and I was given his room.

In Swansea the rehearsals with the band were going well and we had a number of gigs organised under the name Malvin Bishop's Originals. The first was at the Rock & Fountain in Morriston and it went well and was full of old school friends. The second was the cause of some problems and heartache. I was just getting ready to go to the gig at the LA pub in Hafod, Swansea when my mum cornered me. She told me she wasn't happy about me playing in a pub, especially locally. Looking back now, it must have been a very tough pill for her to swallow, seeing her youngest son being a pub singer. It was quite strange for me too. I had been to pubs in Cambridge and London, but I still drank alcohol very rarely. Before this summer I had never been into a pub in Swansea and here I was becoming something of a regular. I tried to explain that this was what I was supposed to do, but it was with a heavy heart I left that night for the gig. The same crowd was there with a few more additional faces swelling the crowd. The band was sounding really tight and inventive and, as a three-piece, it reminded people of the original Elton John band set-up.

It was decided that I would go to London and that the boys would follow as soon as they could. Tony worked at the DVLA which meant leaving behind his pension, Wal was in the process of finishing off a house which he was going to sell to raise money for his new life in the smoke.

With the money from the publishing deal, it was decided that we should record a new set of demos which would be the basis for securing a record deal. Instead of one producer, I would have two. Dennis Weinreich was the staff engineer at Scorpio studios in London and he brought along another American, Howard Massey, who had just had a track covered by Herb Alpert. This was one of those pivotal moments in my life that, given my time again, I would have done very differently. I had a band in Swansea who would die to make a record. The management company had a limited amount of money from my publishing advance to spend on my recordings. I had always been the kid believing that those in the music business who talked loudest with the most confidence where right. This was a painful way to learn that when it comes to making records no one knows any better than you do.

In the meetings prior to the session I kept saying that I wanted to use my band. Dennis was all in favour, but Howard wanted to use tried and tested studio session men. I just remember feeling so disappointed with the sessions. The band were fine but the guitarist had just got a gig with Rick Wakeman and spent most of the session on the phone to his manager. The tracks were OK but, in the meantime, I'd disappointed two of my best friends and spent my advance.

When Pete Brown heard the tracks he was very disappointed and immediately decided he could do a better job himself. He managed to borrow some extra studio time from EMI. Using the same argument as Howard had used, about limited time and the lack of studio experience my band had in Swansea, he put together a band made up of members of After the Fire, the Christian band he had dismissed some months previously, but recently had signed to his management company. The tracks turned out much better and a meeting was arranged with Terry Slater, the guy who had signed me to EMI Publishing and who was now head of A&R at EMI Records. He listened to the tracks and started talking about how the deal would be structured. I walked out of the meeting with Pete and turned to him and asked "Am I right in thinking we've got a record deal with EMI?" Pete turned to me and said "Absolutely!"

I'm not sure when I heard the news that Terry Slater had resigned from EMI Records but the fact that the promised deal never arrived must have started me to question things. So there I was, living in London, signed to Pete and Harvey, going to any gig I wanted to and I was absolutely broke. I still had a strong belief that I was doing what God had called me to do, so I didn't want to give in and either get a proper job or sign on the dole, as both would for me be an admission of failure and would show a lack of faith. I'd got on really well with Dennis Weinreich and we kept in touch during those early London months. I asked him what I should do and he said you've got to hustle! (He was American after all!) And so I hustled. I got a job singing every weekend at a wine bar on the Edgware Road and another at a restaurant called the Click in Chelsea. I also started working at a sports shoe shop on the Kings Road. Will Sloan was one of my best friends at university and he was managing a new shop called Cobra Sports. The shop was owned by two ex-Cambridge hearties who insisted that even their shop assistants should have an Oxbridge degree. Whenever Will was short-handed, he'd give me a call.

Also working at the shop was an Oxford graduate called Jeremy. He wasn't a shoe salesman either, he was an actor. He had a lovely girlfriend called Edwina who would often pick him up at the end of the day. What I loved about Jeremy and Edwina was that you would never have guessed their background if you'd met them in the pub. They were just incredibly friendly, interested in other people and very generous. One evening after work, we were all invited back to Jeremy's house for supper. The walls of the very posh house were covered in photos of famous faces from the royal family and the world of film and television, all inscribed with personal messages of thanks. Jeremy's dad was a doctor and he must have been a pretty good one at that when you considered his clientele. We knew that Edwina was from a pretty well-off family as well, as her grandfather had left her a house somewhere in central London. It was a week or so later that we found out that her grandfather had been Earl Mountbatten.

I was making a living in London but not making much music. I was in the centre of things but nothing was really happening. One day I could be in the office chatting to Billy Connolly (How can the Welsh be funny when their national drink is leek soup!) or going to a Thai restaurant with Mel Smith to join in with him and the Thai waitress in the timeless dance of elegance. Pete was busy with After the Fire. Joining Pete and Harvey was a good move for that band because, through Harvey, they now had access to some of the biggest tours in rock 'n' roll. Over the next year, they would go on to tour with Queen, ELO and Van Halen. Because we had a faith in common as well as management, I would become quite friendly with the band over the coming years. The trouble with After the Fire was that the original deal they signed was so bad that, unless they had a massive worldwide hit, they would never ever really make any money.

But as usual things were starting to come apart at the management company. Pete was becoming very friendly with Mel Smith and Griff Rhys Jones and had been asked to look after their company Talkback, which was specialising in commercials and was planning to move into TV production too. At a meeting Pete and Harvey decided to split and I would join Pete at Talkback. Towards the end of my time with Harvey, the guys form After the Fire invited me to join them for one of the regular prayer meetings, hardly rock and roll I agree. Not all of the members of the band attended, as after years of travelling around the world together, those minor irritations you are bound to feel being cooped up together, had grown into major problems. Also, having given it their best shot and having played to massive audiences supporting bands on Harvey's tours, they were beginning to come to a realisation that they weren't going to crack the big time. Having said all of that, the guitarist John Russell felt a real sense that the Almighty was telling them that their dream was still just around the corner and that if they could just hang on, they would be amazed at what was going to happen. Well, by now, the faith had all but gone and within a couple of months, the band would split up never to reform with the same line-up.

So, I was now signed to Talkback and suddenly I went from being in rooms full of rock stars to rooms full of really clever comedy writers. Afternoons in the company of people like Jimmy Mulville and Rory McGrath were very entertaining, but could also be very intimidating too. In reality, these guys were only a year or so older than me, but I still felt like a kid around them. It was the same feeling of inadequacy that had stopped me getting involved with theatre and comedy in Cambridge. I remember seeing Sandy Toksvig and Emma Thompson performing in end of term review shows and it was always hard not to notice Stephen Fry walking along King's Parade as an undergraduate because he looked so different, but I couldn't find the courage to ask "can I play too?"

In the meantime, Tony and Wal had moved to London under their own steam. Over the coming months they would find new bands to work with. Tony became a member of the Blow Monkeys and Wal joined Gary Numan's band. They were good enough for the studio – they could have been terrific – but no one took the trouble to give us a shot. I was too weak to insist and the moment was lost. It would be another ten years before we would play together.

Chapter 22

Session musician

I'd known a guitarist by the name of Neil Costello for some time. He was from Manchester, but his sister had married a lad from the Gospel Hall in Mumbles and I'd met him through Hilary who went to the same church. He had recently returned from playing in a band in Germany and had spent a couple of days with Tony and Wal in Swansea, before deciding to move to Eastbourne to be near ICC Studios. So it wasn't a complete surprise when he rang me. He was helping to put together a band to back some American Gospel artists throughout the summer and then to go on tour in the autumn. They needed a keyboard player – was I interested? It turned out that one of the artists was Randy Stonehill. He had been at the forefront of the Californian Jesus Music movement and I'd got a couple of his albums in my collection. Playing music and getting paid, that was novel and quite exciting.

I packed up my little green mini and drove to Eastbourne. The band was: Neil on guitar, Dave Engel from Romford on drums and Les Moir on bass. We rehearsed for a week or so and then travelled to Northamptonshire to play at the Greenbelt Festival. 30,000 Christian rock fans, all in a big field together! We were performing two sets. The first was on Saturday, for a very funny guy called Dave Edwards. Randy's set on the Sunday was slightly delayed because an Irish band had dropped by and the organisers wanted them to do a short set. They even had to borrow backline equipment. I had leant Randy my VOX AC 30 and I think the Irish guitarist used the same amp for his set. U2 were always going to be big. They had played a lot of gigs in a lot of small clubs but here, at the festival, they filled the stage. As we were on a little later, I watched them perform from the wings. Bono strutted around the stage like a cockerel on heat, one foot on the monitor in true rock god fashion. It might have been a Christian festival, but the crowd went absolutely wild and I think we all thought to ourselves we had been privileged to see them perform at such close quarters.

Something strange happened before the gig which shook me and also shook Randy. Randy had become a Christian after spending time with Larry Norman. Larry was the godfather of Christian rock music, someone whose songs I had sung for years and who I'd admired even longer. He and Randy had had a disagreement and fallen out. The whole matter was complicated by the fact that when Randy's first marriage broke down, Larry had married his ex-wife. We were headlining on the Sunday night, and it was just starting to get dark as we got changed. Suddenly there was a bit of noise as someone tried to come into our portakabin. It turned out to be Larry. Voices were raised and Larry was asked to leave. All we could hear was Larry speaking in a child-like voice calling Randy's name. It was a little unsettling but, as a band, we got ready and went backstage. It was then that I noticed Larry hiding behind the curtain. I mentioned this to Randy's manager who again escorted Larry away from the stage area. We took our places on stage and Dave counted us into the first song 'Good News'. As Randy walked out to the applause of 30,000 people, it was plain that the only face he saw was Larry's smiling sweetly at him from the VIP enclosure. It was so unsettling that Randy missed his cue to a song he must have sung a million times. Larry stood there for about twenty minutes and then turned and left.

Chapter 23

'I'm going home'

When the Americans left town, it was back to London and the onset of winter, gigs in the wine bar and waiting for something to happen to my career. I'd become good friends with the bass player Les Moir and he bore me in mind when other tours were looking for keyboard players. When we were performing in central London, we would quite often take refuge in the same Salvation Army hostel Elton John had stayed at in his early days as Les's dad, Major Moir, was now the officer in charge. Some of these tours were with recognised musicians like Graham Kendrick, whilst others were more mission-like tours, where we would provide the music for an event which would be headlined by a well-known preacher. For me these were quite strange events. Now from the outside you would have thought one Christian event was much like another, but there are many subtle differences. Maybe it's best illustrated by a joke I was once told by someone brought up in the Plymouth Brethren:

> A believer who has recently died is being shown around Heaven by St Peter. Peter opens one door to see a room full of people dancing and clapping. "That room is for the Pentecostals." He opens another to show a room full of incense and candles. "The Catholics are in there," Peter says. The saint then walks up to the next room and tiptoes past with his fingers to his lips. The new entrant to heaven says "Why are we whispering?" Peter says "That room is for the Plymouth Brethren, they think they are the only ones who got here!"

I'd experienced a little bit of High Church in Cambridge but this was wild. People were falling over left, right and centre as the Spirit moved through the meeting. I was hardly immune from everything I saw but my sense of humour couldn't always be controlled. At one early morning session, we were addressed by a well-known charismatic leader. He asked us all what was the true meaning of the word faith. I raised my hand and said, "Believing in something you know isn't true." Well I thought it was funny, and so did the band but I think some of those in charge felt that maybe I wasn't completely on track with the official party line.

I have always tried to balance my faltering faith with humour, believing that it has a way of cutting away any excess pomposity. But it was back in London that I learnt a very good lesson. I'd been in the presence of miracles for a number of weeks when everyone was encouraged to have a faith that could move mountains. I woke one morning in my little flat in Wealdstone to find frost on the inside of the windows and water pipes frozen so that no water would flow for a cup of tea. Paul, my flatmate, was out, so I decided that I would put into practice everything I'd heard on tour. For the whole day I sat there praying that God would do a miracle and unfreeze the water pipes. I believed and spoke it out loud just the way I'd been told and, do you know what, nothing happened. Around about teatime Paul returned home. I told him we had a problem with frozen pipes and so I couldn't make him a cuppa. Quick as a flash, he got hold of an electric fan heater, opened up the trap door into the attic and pointed the heater at the pipes. Within ten minutes, the water was flowing and the kettle was on. Maybe sometimes God really does want faith that moves mountains but then again sometimes he may just want us to look around at what we have to hand and get on with the job ourselves!

The year stumbled on from tour to shoe shop, from wine bar to days on my own in the flat. Hilary was coming towards the end of her teaching degree and our wedding day was getting closer. We had a look at flats around London, but all seemed to be way out of our price range, especially as I was a musician. I had a chat with Pete Brown, but in all honesty, he couldn't really see anyway forward, as everyone was trying to sign the next Sex Pistols. There was no other option, I would have to put aside the music and see if I could get a job back at the BBC in Cardiff.

CHAPTER 24

Mr and Mrs

I WROTE TO DAVID Nicholas at Radio Wales and explained that, although London had been a great experience, I would really love a job on the *AM* programme. A year earlier, there was a space ready and waiting for me – now the jobs had been filled and it wasn't quite so straightforward. He said he had a couple of weeks of holiday cover in June that I could have and, with that encouragement, I packed up the mini and headed west.

I think everyone was a little concerned that I was getting married at the end of July and had no real prospects. Hilary's parents were very supportive, but I think they had hoped for more when I got into university. The fact that they listened to Chris Stuart every morning on Radio Wales certainly helped. For the first week, I travelled back and forth from Swansea but eventually, through a church connection, I got a flat above a chip shop in Ely, Cardiff. Chris Stuart, the presenter of the show, was very supportive and invited me round to his house to see the opening game of the World Cup when England beat France 3–1, with Bryan Robson scoring after just 27 seconds. I really felt I had landed on my feet.

The work was going well and two weeks turned into a month. As the wedding approached, I was finding it hard to concentrate on the job and preparations. One afternoon, I got a call from Hilary's dad. He wasn't very impressed that I hadn't sorted out the passports. With my lack of forethought it was now too late to get a joint passport in our married name. We could apply for temporary passports, but these would be in the names we had currently on our birth certificates. Hilary would go on honeymoon as a Davies, not a Pope, and they weren't happy about that at all.

David Nicholas said he was sure there would be more work when I got back from my honeymoon and that I was not to worry. And with a big send off from the *AM* staff, I left for Swansea. The wedding day itself couldn't have gone more smoothly. My grandmother played the organ. My brother Gareth was best man. Hilary's uncle Gwilym conducted the service and married us and Hilary's dad was the official registrar who did all of the legal work. It really was a family affair. After a lovely reception at Swansea University we set off in our little green mini to the new world as a married couple. Our wedding night was spent in a lovely country house hotel that specialised in Welsh evening or *Hwyrnos* events. All night long, the sound of clog dancing came banging through our bedroom window. Added to that, was the fact that my mum had bought me a new set of pyjamas which Hilary said made me look like Elvis in his Las Vegas period! So our wedding night started with us laughing and I think it's fair to say she hasn't stopped laughing at me since.

The next leg of the honeymoon tour was Weymouth ready for the ferry to France the following morning. We arrived at the Christian guesthouse only to find that they had lost our reservation. All they could offer was two sun loungers in the breakfast room. (This was probably because the stable was already in use!) Strangely Hilary had commented on our way into Weymouth that it was odd to see one guesthouse advertising that it still had rooms at the height of the season, when every other hotel was saying No Vacancies. We turned the car around and drove straight there. It wasn't difficult to see why it wasn't sold out. Faced with that or the second night of our honeymoon in our car, we decided to cut our losses and take the room. We dived under the polyester sheets and crackled until morning!

France was fun and exciting and our only disappointment

was being woken one morning to be told in broken English that our car had been stolen. We rushed outside and were really pleased to find it was still in the car park. It was only on closer inspection that we found the windscreen had been taken off. We then thought they might have been disturbed as they tried to take the car and that we had got away with a lucky escape. It was only when I went to pay the bill that I couldn't find my wallet. I had left it on the dashboard of the car! We managed to find enough money in Hilary's purse to pay the bill and left for the ferry. We returned home poorer, wiser and with a green mini covered in sticky tape to keep the windscreen in place.

Back in Cardiff, we settled into a bit of a routine. I was starting to produce the early morning show which meant getting up early on production days. It was hard to get out of my musician's body clock but the extra responsibility meant more money. There were no teaching jobs in Cardiff that year, so Hilary got a job in Marks and Spencer. That brought in more cash to the kitty and also meant we ate like kings, as she regularly returned home with some fantastic M&S produce, all just past it's sell-by date.

I was still in regular contact with Pete Brown in London, drawing on my London contacts for interviews on the show and it was via Pete I heard the news that After the Fire had split up. Pete was still good friends with the lead singer Andy Piercy, and he suggested we write some songs together. It wasn't going to be quite as easy, as the radio job was pretty much all consuming, but a little while later I got an envelope full of lyrics from Andy and started to work on them. In the past, my songs had always started with a melody and then I'd try to find lyrics to go with them. This was different and really fast. Andy had been writing lyrics for a long time, so they scanned and had sections which were obviously a chorus or middle eight. It was strange, but as I read the lyrics, the tune seemed to be there already.

November came and through work I was offered tickets to see Elton John at St David's Hall. Hilary and I went along and it was just like the old days. At the end of the show I went to the sound desk and saw Clive Franks, Elton's sound man and engineer on my sessions. He was really pleased to see us, and invited us backstage to see Elton and the band. Elton was lovely, kissed me and Hilary and stopped to chat. He said "stay in touch" and then flew out of my world for another fifteen years. Hey I didn't mind. I had a job I loved, a lovely wife and I was still writing songs. Life was good after all.

We spent Christmas at home in Swansea with the families. It was early in the New Year that Andy Piercy came to stay at the flat in Cardiff and we knocked out some rough demos on his small Sony Walkman recorder. About a month later, I managed to get a few days off from work and travelled down to the studio in Eastbourne to do some demos of the songs. Although After the Fire hadn't been a massive success, Andy was still being managed by Harvey Goldsmith and now, as a solo artist and the lead singer of the band, there was interest from a couple of labels to see what he would come up with next. The sessions went well and the songs we'd written sounded good to me. I didn't expect too much to happen and with the radio production going well, I wasn't particularly interested in getting back on the rock 'n' roll rollercoaster, but it felt good to keep my hand in. And then it happened, after years of struggling, After the Fire had a massive worldwide hit.

Sometimes records can become hits despite of everything, rather than because of what you have done. I'm reminded of a story told to me by Eric Wiesberg, the guitarist who had a hit with the theme 'Duelling Banjos' from the film *Deliverance*. We spent a lot of time together travelling when he was in Art Garfunkel's band and I was the support artist in the late Nineties. Eric had strived for years for a hit, but made his living as a session man. He was asked to go to the south to record a track in a gas station to be used in a new film. A year later, he'd gone to a studio for another session and one of the musicians said he'd heard his record that morning on the radio. "What record?" was Eric's reply. The story was that the film company had made some copies of his performance of 'Duelling Banjos', and had sent it out in a promotion pack for the film. DJs started playing the song and then people started calling in to ask what it was. Within six weeks, the record was number one on the Billboard charts and has helped fund Eric's love of sports cars ever since.

The song 'Der Kommissar' had been a hit in German for an artist called Falco. After the Fire had spent a lot of time in Europe and had heard the song and decided to do a cover. They needed someone to translate it into English but in the end Andy wrote an English lyric keeping the title as the song's hook. The single slipped out in the US and bit by bit, it picked up stations across the country. Within a month or so, it was a Top Five hit in America. I found myself in a very odd situation. I was excited by the prospect of writing songs with a friend who now had a hit in the US, but I knew our material was very different to the original After the Fire sound. Logically, it made sense to get the band back together and CBS, together with Harvey Goldsmith, tried their best but to no avail. Sometimes the pain is stronger than the desire for success.

With no reformed band, CBS did the next best thing which was sign up Andy Piercy. Andy took the name After the Fire or ATF as they became and started work on a new album to follow up the success in the States. Initially, Andy re-recorded a couple of older songs for follow up singles, but it was obvious he needed to record a new album and the only new songs he had were ours.

Chapter 25

'I'm gonna join a Rock 'n' Roll Band'

WHAT HAD STARTED WITH a couple of songs above a chip shop in Cardiff was soon going to become another chapter in the rock 'n' roll book of triumph and disaster. With the success of the single, Andy Piercy was hot and CBS wanted to make him a star. We were booked into Ridge Farm residential studios for a month and there was no expense spared.

I was faced with all sorts of problems. I was newly married and had just moved into a small semi in Cardiff which, at £23,000, cost a small fortune each month in mortgage payments. Hilary had just got a job managing a gift shop and I was getting on pretty well at the BBC. But here I was being offered the chance of a lifetime. I talked it through with Hilary and although scared, she stood right behind my decision. The next step was to talk to my boss Megan Emery. Megan had always been supportive but this was a big request. I wanted to take all of my holiday allowance in one go, so that I could run away to join a rock 'n' roll band. With a bit of manoeuvring she managed to get me two weeks and with that I set out for Ridge Farm.

Ridge Farm was part of the rock dream. A residential studio set in thirteen acres with a recording studio in a barn dating back to the seventeenth century. Everything was provided, from catering to tennis courts. Even if I wasn't going to be a star, at least I was going to be well-fed on my two week holiday. The whole experience was slightly surreal, as musicians came and went as Andy and the producer John Eden looked for the illusive sound of a hit album. First in was the Eric Clapton rhythm section: Dave Markee on bass and Welshman Henry Spinetti on drums. I loved Henry. In between takes he told wonderful stories such as the time when he got a call from an old guitarist friend of his who told him he had met a great new songwriter who was a teacher from Newcastle. They were going on the road and would Henry consider being the drummer. "What's the singer's name?" asked Henry. "Sting and we're going to call the band The Police" said the guitarist Andy Summers. I think it still hurt Henry a bit telling me the story.

With a couple of tracks on tape, a new section was brought in. As this was going to be a big record, everyone thought it would be good to get some guest names in. When Roger Taylor from Queen arrived I tried to be cool, honest I did. I didn't ask for an autograph although I did pinch one of his signature drumsticks at the end of the session. I was a little more confident in my piano playing compared with the Elton John sessions some five years earlier, but I have to say that I did feel a fair amount of pressure every time the red light came on.

Hilary managed to get some time off work to join us at Ridge Farm and when we weren't eating or recording, we were playing tennis or snooker. Harvey Goldsmith came down to the studio with the head of CBS and, having heard the tracks, a decision was made. CBS was moving into CD production. They needed a big album to lead the way. This new project would be the ideal launch vehicle. It was just too good to be true. Andy's management had also been talking to Pete about the future. Plans were afoot to tour again. When the album came out, it would mean basing ourselves in America because we'd be on tour for about 5 months. I remember walking through the streets of Cardiff waiting for the appropriate time to tell Hilary about the plans. I think there were tears as we thought about leaving behind family and friends but it sounded too good to miss. It sounded too good to be true and it was.

I wasn't getting paid to record the album by anyone, this was a big budget album but as co-writer I was expected to be there. At least I'd have a big publishing advance. I was offered a new deal by Andy Piercy's publishers with an advance of about £5,000 per song on the album. I did some quick calculations, that was about £60,000. Then, it all started to unravel. Firstly, it appeared that for some reason no one had checked my last publishing deal. The option period was technically up but when they got wind of the new project some clause was used to tie me in to EMI. They said they would match the MCA offer but any old advances would be brought into the equation. £60,000 became £40,000.

Then the project itself started to lose its way. I think Andy must have been under incredible pressure to follow up his American success. This was his chance at the title and like every prize fighter, he wanted it all. Bit by bit we seemed to lose contact. By this stage I was back in work with no holidays left and I was still being asked to travel back and forth to London to complete work on the record. It finally came to a head late one Sunday evening. I had driven up after work on Friday to do some piano overdubs and backing vocals. Saturday came and went and at Sunday teatime I decided I'd had enough. Hilary and I got in our mini and drove west leaving the project behind. I think it took some time for them to realise what had happened. The following couple of weeks I left the phone on answer phone and didn't return the calls. It sounds childish now but like any close relationship, small events and slights can grow to the point where everyone starts to act unreasonably.

I decided I would concentrate on the radio production and put the other dreams aside. When the CD and record were released, I was going to get quite a big publishing advance anyway so I thought I would bide my time and let things work themselves out. But the record never was released and I never got a penny from any publisher. I wasn't the only one who had become disillusioned. It later became apparent that Andy and the producer weren't seeing eye-to-eye. The album went way over budget and over time and missed the kudos of being CBS's first CD release. Eventually, all that was released was a co-written single called '8 Ball in the Top Pocket' and I only found that out when the record came in to the BBC one morning on the new releases schedule. It would be some time before Andy and I would speak and even longer before we were completely reconciled but I put it all down to experience and decided to move on.

CHAPTER 26

First it's TV – then it's back to music

IT WOULD HAVE BEEN difficult not to be disappointed by the experience, but work at the BBC was going well and there's nothing like a little success to encourage you in your work. I had been lent Andy's old Tascam Portastudio, a 4-track cassette machine, to record some of the tunes we'd been working on and somewhere along the line, Andy had said he'd bought a new one, so I could hang onto it. I started buying some drum machines and synthesisers and with Hilary's blessing, turned the spare bedroom into a little studio.

Chris Stuart's star at the BBC was still rising and he'd been offered a new chat show. Because of my showbiz background, I was offered the job as researcher. It meant leaving the safety of Radio Wales, but again I was looking forward to a new challenge. The series took a while to plan and introduced me to the world of broadcasting politics. Radio is, in reality, a fairly straightforward medium. You can make a programme anywhere with very little equipment. Television is a completely different game with everything having to be planned to the last detail because it involves so many people. It took a while to understand the machinations of the TV machine, but I really enjoyed the experience, especially the excitement in the studio on recording days.

It was around this time that I got involved in a small project which would eventually come to define me. I just need to jump forward 25 years to my college reunion at Christ's College, Cambridge. I walked into the Fellow's garden and heard friends calling to each other things like, "Hi John, are you still at the Treasury?" Conversation could be heard of how successful everybody's life had been over the intervening years. One had published *Bridget Jones' Diary*; another had become a world leader in Physics; another was on the board of the biggest firm of accountants in the world. What I noticed was over the course of the two days; one by one, each of my college friends would sidle up to me and ask, "Did you really sing *Fireman Sam*?"

I had already sung a number of theme songs for cartoons starting off with *Superted* which had been written by Chris Stuart. That had led to a number of demos for series that would never see the light of day, which had either been written or produced by a team of mad boffin-type musicians working under the collective title of Heneghan and Lawson. They had a strange way of working together which always seemed to be in a state of flux or conflict, which never really became aggressive but always made me feel any moment something was going to blow – which it never did, incidentally. It was just the way they worked. I got a call from the boys saying they'd been asked to write the theme music for a new cartoon being produced by S4C about a Welsh fireman; could I help them out with a demo? I drove over to Ian's house, where they had a little studio set up in their bedroom. The song was really clever and I had the chance to do a lot of backing vocals as well. News came back that the boys had got the gig and we recorded a version in English and Welsh and also a full-length song version too. So, I signed the contract with S4C, collected my one-off payment and forgot about the show. Well, it was just a kids TV show and I was sure the whole thing would be forgotten in a year or so!

As well as working and fitting in the odd session in the evening, I started writing and recording again and before too long I had a new collection of songs. There is a definition of insanity which is 'doing the same thing over and over and expecting different results'. Maybe the definition sums up what it means to be a musician. My insanity meant I would again send a tape to Jeff Griffen at Radio 1. A couple of weeks later, Jeff replied saying he liked the new songs and would like to play them out on the Andy Peebles show as they were for their 'in session' series. I was delighted and the week was pencilled in for a month or so in the future.

The *Chris Stuart Cha Cha Chat Show* meant that I was researching and booking guests as diverse as John Humphrys, the newsreader to Terry Griffiths, the world snooker champion, to Basil Brush! The producer of the show had a stammer and so we were never sure if that was the correct name for the series or whether it had just been a slip of the tongue at a crucial planning meeting. Whatever the real reason, it became the show's title as everyone was too afraid to ask for clarification.

We always tried to get an unusual mixture of guests for the show. One of the most interesting shows was when the line-up included the singer Dorothy Squires and football man John Toshack OBE. Dorothy Squires had, at one time been the highest-paid female entertainer in Britain and her marriage to Roger Moore and her love affair with the British legal system had made her a household name. When she was a guest on the show, her professional life was in the doldrums, but she still behaved and acted like the star she had been. On the day of the show, it was my job to look after the guests, making sure they had everything they needed and also to introduce them to the other guests on the show. I remember introducing her to John Toshack in the Green Room. She was looking fabulous, all hair, make up and sparkling jewellery. She was a fairly short lady and, standing next to Toshack, the difference in height was even more apparent. I said, "Ms Squires, this is John Toshack." She took his hand and stared up at him. "You're an actor aren't you," she said, to which Toshack replied, "Sometimes, only sometimes."

She arrived at the studio with an entourage and an

enormous bouquet of flowers which, on her cue, I had to rush onto the TV set to present to her during the interview. I did as requested and she cried in front of the cameras as she showed how overwhelmed she was at this spontaneous action from the BBC! My appearance on set was subsequently cut from the actual broadcast show, but I couldn't help but feel I'd had real brush with real old-fashioned show business that night.

Another of the guests that left quite an impression was Mandy Rice Davies. She had become a national figure when her friendship with Christine Keeler and a number of members of the British establishment was brought to the public's attention when John Profumo, the Minister of War resigned from the government in 1963. By the early 1980s, she was well on her "descent to respectability" but she had a remarkable power to entrance anyone she met, particularly men. Mandy Rice Davies shared the show with a very pretty young singer named Jade.

I was also responsible for finding musical guests and when a new single from a Welsh singer called Jade from Tonypandy came in, I suggested we had her on the show. The producer agreed and I started speaking to her manager Larry Page. Larry Page's family came from Neath but he had been born Lenny Davies in Middlesex. In the Fifties he became a singer and, realising he needed a new name to rival his competitors like Billy Fury and Vince Eager, he settled on Larry Page and soon took on the strap line, the Teenage Rage. Everyone needed a gimmick and Larry chose to wear oversized heavy-framed glasses.

After his solo career came to an end, Larry moved into music production and management and looked after The Kinks and Troggs during their most successful years. Larry had continued making records and had found Jade, a young singer from Wales. Larry was old school. He had been close friends with the Tin Pan Alley music-men, especially Dick James. He had also known Elton in his Reg Dwight days. I booked Jade for the show and got on well with Larry on the phone. I tried to keep my music separate to the TV show, but when he came down for the day's recording in the studio, my connection to Elton came out and he said he remembered a kid with a strange Welsh name. That kid was me. I told him about the new Radio 1 session and he asked for a copy. I sent him a cassette and Larry phoned asking me why I wasn't making records. We chatted for sometime and he said he would like to manage me. I couldn't see any harm in letting him try to place the songs with a publisher and with my expectations low, I carried on with my TV job.

A couple of weeks passed before Larry called again. He had played the songs to Granada publishing and they wanted to sign my publishing and were prepared to pay me an advance of £6,000 which went up £1,000 every year for the following two years.

Life was further complicated by the fact that the family was all set to grow, I was going to be a dad. We were delighted and, with Hilary's dad being very unwell following a stroke, the news was a great boost for all of the family. With my family being notorious worriers, we decided to wait until the contract was signed before announcing to them that I was leaving the BBC and going back to being a professional musician. They did their best to look pleased but worry does have a powerful control over facial muscles.

We sold up in Cardiff and moved back to Swansea. My TV researcher's contract with the BBC Wales had finished but I kept my connection with Radio Wales, popping back when they need production cover in the mornings. But my main concern now was writing new songs and starting to work on new recordings with Larry. The new house had three bedrooms, so one was taken for a nursery and the spare became my new home studio. I was still picking up session work in studios as far away as Eastbourne, Hereford and London which kept my name in the frame for various gigs as we prepared for recording a new album in Stoke-on-Trent. Larry had a friend with a studio in Hanley and so began a regular trek to the Midlands. As well as working on my album, I also started writing songs for Jade and also followed up any leads from the publisher.

The progress was slow but positive and Larry was always great for a story or two. He had been with the Kinks and Troggs at the height of their Sixties careers, being responsible for some of their biggest hits. I got the impression that the Troggs had been a delight and the Kinks were more of a trial. Larry told me about the time he'd been approached by the Mafia in the US with a view to him working for them. He said that after a show in Las Vegas with the Kinks, he'd been invited to take a journey with a well-known 'wise guy' in a limousine. "I like you," the mobster said to Larry. "I like you and I want to give you a publishing company and then maybe we can work together." Denmark Street in London might have been full of dodgy characters and dealings, but this was the real thing. Larry said the first thing he did was to thank him for the company, but then told him that he liked working alone. The mobster looked at him for a little while, told him he still liked him, dropped him off at the hotel and never bothered him again. But it wasn't the Mafia that forced him out of the US, it was the Kinks. After one more bust-up with the band, following on from a series of bust-ups, Larry was faced with a full Hollywood Bowl and Ray Davies refusing to go on stage. This was the last straw for Larry, who made sure they were paid, got a cab to the airport and flew home.

My second year's publishing option was taken up, including an increase of £1,000. Larry and I continued to work on various projects. Larry had high hopes that contacts he'd made in previous years would soon bear fruit for me and Jade and Larry's contacts were indeed first division. It was he who had introduced Sonny to Cher, as well as Clive Davis, the legendary head of Arista, who had just had another worldwide success with Whitney Houston. Then, fate played a totally unexpected card. Larry hadn't really spoken to Ray Davies or the Kinks for years. In fact it had been nearly twenty years and then it had ended in court. Out of the blue, Ray had rung Larry and asked if he'd be interested in managing him again. Ray had just had a big hit with a song called 'Come Dancing' and he needed help. The fact that Ray had come back made Larry feel vindicated by the position he taken twenty years previously. Also, Larry thought the new connection could only help his other projects.

As the year dragged on, Ray seemed to take more of Larry's time and energy and doors which we thought might open for Jade and me stayed firmly shut. It's hard to tell exactly when a moment has passed, but the feeling was things weren't going to go much further. The second year ended on the publishing deal and Granada came back to me saying that they weren't going to take up the next option as it stood, but that they would take a year's extension with a much reduced advance. This was pretty devastating news, as we had been banking on the money and our second child was on the way. Even though we were desperate, I thought the songs were worth more than their offer. So I turned down their offer and thought it best if Larry and I parted too, so that I could start again. Larry was fine and understood which was very fair, I thought.

In the agreement with Granada, songs which had not been recorded a certain amount of time after being assigned to the company, could be returned to me. I checked the dates and started to ask for songs to be returned. Two songs right at the start of the term were 'Reunion Of The Heart' and 'This Is It'. 'Reunion Of The Heart' had been inspired by a letter from friends in Newcastle who felt they had a word for me from on high. It had sounded like a good song title to me and was one of those songs that wrote itself. One evening, I was sitting at home when I got a call from Les Moir, the bass player from the gospel touring days. He had been travelling in a car with Cliff Richards's publisher Stuart Ongley, and had played him a tape of songs we had recorded in the Eastbourne days, which included 'Reunion Of The Heart'. Cliff's publisher wanted to know who owned the song. A couple of days earlier it had belonged to Granada, but now it was mine. He was also quite keen on the 'This Is It' song as well. It was common knowledge in the business that a track on a Cliff album was worth a lot of money. In my head I'd already spent it!

It wasn't long after the contract ended that I started asking for my copyrights back. Then I got a call from Granada. They had sent some of my songs to the Hollies who were looking for new material for their new album, which was being recorded to celebrate their silver anniversary. They really liked two songs, 'Reunion Of The Heart' and 'This Is It'. What on earth was I going to do? I had two artists I had known all of my life, both wanting to record the same songs. I sort of ignored it for a while thinking that one or the other was bound to fall through. In the meantime, I started working in a little studio in Swansea which was based in the back of a van. Black Mountain Records specialised in location recording of choirs and in the downtime the studio was housed in a lock-up garage. I started doing some producing there and eventually moved in. The owner of the studio, Mike Evans, had some publishing connections and had sent some new songs I had written to Carlin Music. They had particularly liked one of the songs called 'Everybody'. Without my knowledge, they had entered the song into the annual *Song for Europe* competition. As the weeks went past, the song made it through round after round. 1987 looked as if it might be the most exciting year ever.

CHAPTER 27

1987 Eurovision, Cliff, the Hollies… this must be the year

I KNEW SOMEWHERE ALONG the line that I'd have to get tough. The Granada publisher had sent the songs to the Hollies, of that there was no doubt, and here he was asking me to reassign the songs to them. But I was an unemployed father of one, with another on the way, and not one but two internationally successful artists wanted to record them. It was a difficult phone call with a lot of silences from the London side, but I had to think of my family.

Then I had to speak to Cliff Richard's publisher. He wanted to publish the songs which Cliff was about to record. It was around this time that I heard from various sources that Cliff's new album project had taken a new turn. A new producer, Alan Tarney, had been brought in and he was going to write all of the songs for the album. No one had told me directly, but it looked like my big cheque from Cliff was starting to get smaller. I was upset to say the least, so I said I was going to hang onto the publishing myself. Threats of legal proceedings started being bandied about and, as someone once told me, where there's a hit there's a writ. In the end I compromised and signed the publishing of 'Reunion Of The Heart' to Cliff's company and held on to the other myself.

The first release was 'This Is It' by the Hollies. Hilary and I were invited to their anniversary concert at the Albert Hall. They went through all of their hits from 'Bus Stop' to 'Carrie Ann' to a couple of songs they had covered written by Bruce Springsteen. They sang both of my songs and I was ecstatic. For the songs to be in such company was very pleasing and there was a great response from the Albert Hall audience. The single was played on Radio 2 and also had a couple of TV performances too, but it wasn't a hit. I was slightly disappointed, but the year seemed to have so many opportunities, something was bound to break.

It was early spring when the news came through that my song 'Everybody' had made it through to the last ten songs and would feature in the *Song for Europe* televised final. There was an awful lot to be organised in a short space of time. The song had been recorded as a demo with me playing everything and singing all of the backing vocals. In 1987 the rules were such that you couldn't use a backing track, everything had to be performed live. We would be provided with a full orchestra and that would be directed by the legendary TV composer and arranger Ronnie Hazlehurst. The first thing was to get the song scored out for an orchestra. It might seem strange, but I don't actually write music down onto paper. My mum always said I'd regret giving up music theory lessons and at this time she was proved right. The only thing I could think of was to ask a favour from my favourite music boffins Heneghan and Lawson. By this time *Fireman Sam* had become quite a hit on children's television and they were more than willing to take my tape and turn it into a full orchestral score.

I also realised that just having me sat at a piano wouldn't be very Eurovision, so I decided that I would ditch the piano and just stand there and sing. To that, I added three girl backing singers. I'd known Cheryl and Sheila Parker for years. The Parker sisters were two beautiful girls who sang like angels. They had been performing together almost since they could talk and singing in harmony was second nature to them. Lorraine Thorne was also a good friend who I'd met through a guitarist friend of mine called Peter King. He thought she would be the perfect third member of the backing vocal group and he was right.

The hook of the song was a line played on a harmonica. On the record it was actually a synthesizer but for the television performance I knew we had to have the real thing. How do I describe Paul Henry without using the term legend? Paul had been born into a Swansea showbiz family and had been playing harmonica for years. Larry Adler described him as his finest pupil and he really did have the music world at his fingertips. But Paul was and is different. He discovered surfing at an early age and living on the beach in Caswell on Gower meant he had ample opportunity to spend his days in the water. The rest of the summer would be spent driving at high speed around the narrow Gower lanes in his red Ferrari sports car. In the winter months he would become a snowbird, flying south to Marbella to perform a Jerry Lee Lewis tribute act in the clubs along the harbour. Luckily, he was back for the spring and was delighted to be a part of the team.

Mike Evans from Black Mountain organised a Swansea nightclub for our rehearsals and with the girls taking control of the choreography, we rehearsed our moves. I was still producing Chris Stuart for Radio Wales at the time. There was a strict embargo on the songs featured in the final, but that didn't stop Radio Wales following me in the build-up to the show. In the weeks leading up to our first television appearance, I became a regular guest on the *AM* programme, telling them how the dance routines were going, what we were going to wear and what publicity activities I'd been up to in the previous week. It was also an opportunity to talk about my other musical activities. Cliff Richard's project had gone very quiet but the Hollies were just about to release their second single 'Reunion Of The Heart'. Once again it picked up quite a lot of radio play and the odd TV show as well, but after a week or so it was obvious that the Hollies weren't going to be back in the UK charts anytime soon. Two chances down – well there was always Eurovision.

My Eurovision song 'Everybody' was premiered on the

Wogan show on April Fool's Day! Terry Wogan presented an early evening chat show on BBC 1 when there were only four terrestrial channels. It had one of the highest regular audiences of any entertainment show on television and you could guarantee that at any one time, there would be fifteen million plus people watching the programme. Mike Evans hired a transit van and we drove to the BBC's Shepherd's Bush theatre in London. Mike had managed to organise a sponsorship deal with the local Top Shop. I was in dressed in tight blue jeans and a white jacket, complete with Dynasty-style padded shoulders which looked as if it had been designed for a fairly large ice cream salesman. I had enormous 'Buggle' style glasses and a new haircut, courtesy of local hairdressers Visage in Swansea! The girls were in identical salmon-pink puff-ball skirts, matching jackets and lacy gloves. Paul Henry wore a suit with enormous checks which looked two sizes too big for him. As I write this, I am watching the performance on *youtube*. The girls still look great but Paul and I look vaguely ridiculous. At the time we thought we looked the business.

The first person I spoke to when we got there was the musical director Ronnie Hazlehurst. He was more than pleased with the score provided by Heneghan and Lawson and, after the normal formalities, we gathered around him at the front of the orchestra to have a run through. I had been to recording sessions where string sections had been added, but this was completely different as everything was there all at the same time, drums, bass guitars. With the girls singing and Paul on harmonica, it was magical. Ronnie seemed impressed with the performance, complimented the girls and turned to Paul Henry. Ronnie was famous for writing the theme music to *Last of the Summer Wine* which also featured a harmonica. "Do you read?" asked Ronnie. This was a big moment for Paul. I thought there can't be too many harmonica players around as good as Paul and this looked like an open invitation to Paul to join the big league. Paul thought for a moment raised his hands as if in surrender and said "Only the Beano, man!"

The theatre was wonderful, quite small but full of stories and ghosts. This had been the home of *Crackerjack* and Esther Rantzen's *That's Life* shows which I had grown up with. Our performance went well and I was really very pleased with the way everyone coped with the pressure. I have to say Terry Wogan kept himself pretty much to himself. I suppose it would have been difficult to be too overtly friendly. The only time we came close to bumping into him was when we overheard him in his dressing room tell his assistant that he was slipping out the back way, to avoid the marauding Welsh who had taken over the building!

After all of the build-up, the climax was a live show on a Friday evening. We travelled up in the transit on the Wednesday for rehearsals. Paul and the girls were so naturally funny that they made the whole crew fall in love with us. For them it was just a bit of fun, a couple of days out in London. For me it was a little bit more serious, with one child and another on the way, winning would make a big difference to us as a family. Maybe it was because our group charmed the people working on the show, but everyone seemed to think we had a really good chance of winning.

Hilary was noticeably pregnant by now and travelled up to London for the show with friends from church, Brian and Ali Farr. I remember standing in the dressing room prior to taking to the stage. I realised that this was either the last time I would sing 'Everybody' or it would be the start of singing it every night of my life. Well, it turned out to be the last time. The show went smoothly. We were shocked to see the group before us ending their song with our signature raising our hands to the sky move. They hadn't done that in rehearsals. Then we took our place on stage and sang our hearts out. I actually looked like a manic version of Brains from *Thunderbirds* with my staccato dance moves, but no one could say we didn't give it our best shot. As the scores came in from panels around the country, our Eurovision dream disappeared. Even the Welsh jury didn't give us full marks. I often say that we came last, which isn't quite true but when the cameras went to the final placing there weren't many songs below us. I had said that all along it was just a bit of fun, a lottery, but I was devastated. We were all invited to the after-show party, but in the end I decided to take the short journey to Paddington with Hilary and take a long silent train ride home.

CHAPTER 28

Max Boyce changed my life!

OVER THE FOLLOWING WEEK or so, I learnt a very hard lesson; it goes very quiet very quickly when you are not the winner. I had been busy every day up to the final, making plans and arrangements, rehearsals and photo sessions. I came home to silence. Hilary tried her best to cheer me up but I was very low. It was just a couple of days later I got an unexpected call. “Hello is that Mal?” said a very soft Welsh voice. “Yes,” I answered. “It’s Max here... Max Boyce.” In my life there was only one Max and he really didn’t need to clarify it. “I’m doing a tour of Hong Kong, Korea, Australia and New Zealand. I need a keyboard player, would you be interested?”

I didn’t know what to say. I asked if I could think about it and ring him back. My name had been put forward by my friend the guitarist Peter King who had been playing for Max for sometime. The rest of the band was Swansea boys I knew well, Paul Smith on drums and Paul Carmen on bass. I rang Pete and he said we’d have great fun. I spoke to Hilary and explained it would mean being away for about six weeks. She would be left at home with a two-year-old and with another on the way. The strange thing is that when you have a bit of success, like we apparently had by reaching the Song for Europe final, everybody thinks you are too busy to work and the phone goes very quiet. Whether we liked it or not, finances meant that I would have to join the Max Boyce band on a tour halfway around the world, and the smile was back on my face.

Preparations included a day or so with the boys running

through songs that Max usually did in concert. "When's Max going to join us for a rehearsal?" I kept asking, only for the other boys to laugh every time. We travelled to Gatwick by train and met Max and his manager Stuart Littlewood at the check-in desk. They were accompanied by a big loud northerner called Bill Thompson, who was responsible for the Hong Kong and Korean legs of the tour. The reason we were then heading on to Australia and New Zealand was that Max had carefully planned his tour to coincide with the inaugural Rugby World Cup. As always, he wanted to say I was there.

Apart from my flight to Manchester as a kid, this was my first real long-haul flight and it was great. Max, Stuart and Bill were in first class and we were in economy, but it didn't matter. We watched films, ate the meals and worked our way through the cocktails list on the Cathay Pacific menu. Every so often Max would come to see us bringing with him a copy of their menu to show what we were missing! After eight hours we stopped in Dubai and after walking around with our naïve Welsh eyes wide open, staring at the gold and people in Bedouin clothing, we hopped back on the plane for another eight hours. I remember staring out of the windows as we flew over the mountains of China and being filled with an incredible sense of awe. My faith was all well and good in the comfortable surroundings of family and home, but looking out of the window I was struck by the immensity of it all. I sat back in my seat and started to think long and hard about the meaning of life.

We arrived at Hong Kong's Kai Tak airport in the morning. It was a tricky airport to land at as the pilot had to fly over a mountain and then descend very quickly, flying though the skyscrapers to set the plane down on the runway which jutted out into Victoria Harbour. As we flew past the buildings, it felt as if we could almost reach out and touch the washing that was drying on the balconies of the apartments we passed.

We got off the plane and were hit by the heat and humidity. It was like a very warm greenhouse. The other thing was the smell. I'm not sure whether it was being so close to the sea or whether it was the spices in the air. Maybe, as James Clavell describes in his book *Noble House* which is set in Hong Kong, it was the smell of money. Whatever it was, I knew I was somewhere very different and I was excited.

We were based at the Harbour View Hotel which lived up to its name with a spectacular view of Victoria Harbour. I was sharing with Peter King which always led to some wise cracks. When we asked for our names at reception he was down on the list as P. King! Although we had travelled for nearly a whole day, we couldn't wait to get out and explore and the city was beyond my imagination. It had the trappings of British colonial heritage with red buses and British police officers. As part of our deal we were able to eat at the hotel and their restaurant reflected the fact that Hong Kong sat on the crossroads of the world; it had a buffet which featured food from every corner of the planet. The choice was incredible, indescribable, sometimes inedible and often unknown. I decided that, as this was a trip of a lifetime, I would try every thing once. Not everyone felt the same way. Paul Smith the drummer had a rather limited palate when it came to food. While the rest of the band was eating a wide selection of some of the best food the world had to offer and all for free, Paul was out spending his per diems at the local Wendy burger restaurant.

Our first gig was at the hotel itself with an audience full of ex-pats. I still hadn't gone through any of the songs with Max but that didn't seem to matter. Our support artist was Eve Graham, formerly of the New Seekers, and we had the chance to rehearse with her during our sound check. The evening was a great success and we spent the rest of the night talking to homesick Welsh people. Over the coming days, we played at the exclusive Hong Kong Golf Club and the even more exclusive Hong Kong Club. After one of our gigs, we went to the downstairs lounge of the Harbour View hotel. The Filipino band was turning out near perfect copies of Lionel Richie songs. At the end of their set, they came to join us at our table and we told them how good we thought they were. The Filipino drummer asked us where we were from. We said "Britain." "Where in Britain?" "It's on the west coast, a country called Wales." Then he wanted to know north or south. We said "South." "Cardiff?" "No, Swansea." "Ah, my wife comes from Trewyddfa Road," he said with the slightest Welsh accent seeping through. Ray had met a Swansea girl in Hong Kong, married her and had dreams of playing in the UK. The next time I saw him was at a gig in Swansea some years later.

On the 18th of May we played at the China Fleet Club, the home of the British Forces in Hong Kong. I don't know why I should have expected anyone to know it was my birthday, but the longer the day went on the more miserable I got. We packed down our gear and Peter phoned home only to be asked how had Mal's birthday been? Peter told the band, the band told Max and we were off.

Bill Thompson was an old Hong Kong hand and knew all of the late-night clubs in Hong Kong. We walked the street for a while until we came to an underground Vietnamese Karaoke Bar. We all walked in and got some strange looks from the other club members. In the corner was a Hammond organ and on all of the tables were song books with lyrics in English, Cantonese, Mandarin and Vietnamese. Drinks and chips were ordered all round and we joined a table with a lot of very friendly Chinese girls. Eventually we got our turn to sing. Firstly Eve Graham took the mike and I played 'I'd Like to Teach the World to Sing' for her. Then Max undid his shirt, told everyone that he was Tom Jones and sang 'The Green, Green Grass of Home'. By this stage there was no stopping us as we went through 'Calon Lân', 'Bread of Heaven' and every Welsh hymn we could remember. I could definitely see the locals were getting a bit annoyed at us hogging the show. It was early in the hours of the following morning that we stumbled up the stairs of the club, walked back to the hotel and fell into bed.

The following morning was an early start and we met in the lobby ready to check-out as we had a plane to catch to South Korea. We were all a bit bleary eyed but still laughing about the party which had finished just a couple of hours earlier. Someone said "What did you think of those Chinese whores we met last night?" I must admit I didn't laugh. Winnie and her friends – the evening before – whores? How could I have been so naïve and stupid? Of course they weren't there to party, they were there to work. Instead of getting hit on, we'd spoken to them, bought them chips and sung with them. They hadn't made any money, but at least they had laughed a lot. Then I got to thinking about Jesus and how he spent all of his time in the company of publicans and sinners. I got to thinking how easily these girls would have been condemned back home. I hadn't knowingly ever met a prostitute in my life and here I had spent an evening in their company and enjoyed talking to them. I was on tour with Max Boyce and the world was getting bigger by the moment. The difficult thing was my head, heart and faith were having to stretch to accommodate it.

Chapter 29

Well, Mr Customs Officer: It's like a six-foot spring onion!

THE FLIGHT TO SEOUL was eventful. The turbulence over the East China Sea meant that Peter and I had to hold hands with Smithy the drummer who had turned a very strange shade of yellow. The next problem was the leek. Max took a six-foot fibreglass leek on tour with him, which he carried on stage at the start of his show. The idea was that each of us in turn would take responsibility for taking the leek through customs. I drew the short straw, or should that be big leek, for Seoul. The leek travelled in its own padded case and, of course, as I tried to wheel it through the 'nothing to declare' aisle, I was stopped.

All I remember is seeing the rest of my band mates laughing at me from the other side of immigration as I tried to explain in sign language why I was trying to bring a big spring onion into Korea. They spoke no English, I spoke no Korean. I think in the end they put me down as being a mad Brit and let me through.

Seoul itself was pretty much a building site as they were preparing for the 1988 Olympic Games. Seoul was going to be a very different challenge for Max. Hong Kong was full of British ex-pats, but, as the custom officials proved, there was no knowledge of Max, Wales or giant leeks in the land of the morning calm. We unpacked in a very nice hotel which had telephones in the bathrooms. As you can imagine, much fun was had by all. The gig was at a club for American ex-pats and I wondered how Max would cope. I have to say watching him work that day, I was completely blown away. Most of

Max's act is storytelling and he was able to tailor his stories so that the Americans understood. He threw in tales from his time with the Dallas Cowboys and his time learning to be a Rodeo rider and he nailed it.

The following day we headed back to Hong Kong for our flights to Australia. We arrived at Kai Tak in the middle of the night and the city full of skyscrapers and lights looked like a planet scene from *Dr Who*. We didn't even leave the airport and, after saying our goodbyes to Eve and Bill, we boarded a plane for Sydney. We were met at the airport by the promoter John Nicholls and our tour manager and were taken to our hotel, The Southern Cross, which was in walking distance of the harbour. On our first night in Sydney, Max walked us down to the harbour. We weren't expecting the sights we saw in the red light district of Kings Cross. The Aussies seemed to be much more broad-minded than the Brits with what they allowed to be advertised and I think we were all slightly shocked by the liberal display of bare flesh. Once settled at the restaurant, Max insisted we all ordered oysters Kilpatrick, oysters cooked with bacon and breadcrumbs. They tasted great. As we sat overlooking the harbour, all of us agreed that we liked Australia.

The first leg of the tour wasn't terribly demanding. We spent quite a lot of time drinking Fosters whilst sat around the rooftop pool. Our first gig was at a club in Parramatta, where we performed in cabaret following on from a magician who really did cut his assistant in half and found doves in every pocket of his suit. Max insisted on releasing imaginary doves from his pockets all the way through the show.

Our next show was at the beautiful Sydney State Theatre (not the Opera House). The theatre is a beautiful Art Deco-style building which in my mind was gold and red. The audience was Welsh through-and-through and so started our Welsh cake crawl. Everyone had brought Max Welsh cakes and we were given the leftovers. Part of our job was to be around to talk to the ex-pats after the show. Max often tells this story which I think, from our experience, is based on fact. Max is greeted by a lady at the end of a show in Australia and she complains that hearing him has made her feel so homesick, which is such a shame, as she was just getting used to life away from Wales. Max asks here how long she has been away, and she replies 28 years!

From Sydney we flew to New Zealand. Once airborne, the captain addressed the passengers. He welcomed us aboard the Qantas flight to Wellington. He advised us that there was going to be a time change. "If you'd like to set your watches back 10 years..." We were met at the airport by the New Zealand promoter, Benny the Hat, and taken into Wellington. I'm sure Wellington has changed in many ways since 1987, but the first thing that struck us was that this was where all of the Morris Minors had gone when they disappeared from Britain. Because New Zealand was so far away from anywhere and there was a high tax on cars, the cars that had been brought out by Brits emigrating were being kept on the road for as long as possible. If the city has changed, one thing which I am sure is still the same is the wind. Windy Wellington they call it and as we were in the middle of their winter, it didn't disappoint. The show went well and feeling hungry after the show, Benny the Hat recommended a Chilean restaurant not far from the hotel. We got there and found it almost empty. There was a little stage and the waiters were taking it in turns to play the guitar and sing songs. We ordered a Chilean omelette each and enjoyed the music. As a band, we were all big fans of Linda Ronstadt, who often sang songs in Spanish to pay homage to her Latino roots. We asked if the owner would mind if we gave them a song and with Peter playing guitar, Smithy on bongos, Paul Carmen and me on vocals, we gave them a Linda Ronstadt song 'Lo Siento Mi Vida'. We didn't have a clue what we were singing, but it seemed to have a tremendous effect on the staff who all hugged us at the end of our performance and refused to take any money for our food!

We flew to Auckland for a concert in the city of sails before returning to Sydney. Our next concert was in Canberra. It looked pretty close on the map but the fact it took us nine hours to drive there gave us some idea of the size of the country. From Canberra we headed for Melbourne and then on to Adelaide. The more we saw of the country, the more we fell in love with it and the outdoor lifestyle. I'm sure if it hadn't been for the family ties in Wales, most of us would have stayed.

Our final stop was Perth, the most isolated city in the world. On our last night I thought it would be a good idea to get some presents and I ended up in a toy shop near the hotel. There were some Australian kids there but I was sure the dad sounded Welsh. I nearly walked out but I turned around to go back in and say hello. As I walked up to the dad I recognised him – Dave Allen from St John's Road in Swansea. "Hello Dave," I said "I'm Maldwyn." He nearly fell over. Dave had been older than me, but taken me under his wing when I was a kid. I'd had a bit of a crush on his sister Jan who he then told me was also in Perth. I invited them all to the concert and we all met for a drink in the bar after the show. As this was our final night singing and playing, 'I'm Going Home To Swansea Town' had even greater resonance. It had been a trip of a lifetime and a life changing trip too. I would never be the same after going around the world with Max Boyce but now it was back to Wales and to a diary which was empty. It would be nice to get home but what was I going to do next?

Chapter 30

'What do I do now?'

HILARY HAD DRIVEN UP to Gatwick in time to meet me at the airport and it was a very shy two-year-old Amy Rose that gave me my first hug back in Britain. It took a couple of days to get back onto an even keel. The first thing was to get some work in the diary. An old friend from the gospel music days had been working on a project for some time and it was now coming to fruition. John Paculabo had run one of the most successful Christian music companies, but had decided he wanted to strike out on his own. His idea was to invite people to send in new gospel songs and hymns that they had written for a new hymn book and the project would be called People's Praise. John wanted me to produce the tracks and also write a couple of songs for every release to make up the numbers and balance of the project. What started out as two cassettes ended up as a collection of eight with songs with vocals on one side and the backing tracks without vocals on the other side, so that people could use them in church. It wasn't exactly rock and roll, but it meant Peter King and I could continue working together in the studio.

It was while I was in the planning stages of recording that I got a call from Megan Emery at BBC Wales. They had been pleased with my contributions to their output during the build up to Eurovision and they were wondering if I would be interested in presenting the morning show for a couple of weeks as the regular presenter wanted a holiday. Many years earlier, I had made a demo tape when a position for a continuity announcer had been advertised and that hadn't got anywhere. Here I was being offered a golden opportunity to try to become a presenter.

Roy Noble had been the regular early morning presenter for a number of years. I had known Roy from the beginning. Whilst I was a young researcher on the *AM* programme, we had commissioned Roy to write a regular 'Letter from Aberdare'. He had come to the attention of Dai Nicholas at BBC Wales, having sent him some form of correspondence every day. Sometimes it would be a cut out picture of a muscle-man with the name Roy Noble attached. Sometimes it would be a poem. Eventually intrigued, Dai wrote to Roy and asked him to pop in for a chat. After a while, his potential was spotted and he decided to take a sabbatical from teaching to become a regular presenter. Thirty years later and he still hasn't gone back.

Roy had recently left the early mornings for a later slot, only to be replaced by a funny young man straight out of the Royal Welsh College of Music and Drama named Rob Brydon. Rob at that time was going by the name Rob Jones, but had to change it later when he found that Equity already had someone using that name. Rob was incredibly funny on the air but, to be honest, most of the time it went completely over the audience's heads. As the morning producer I didn't really have any production responsibility for Rob, but as we shared the same studio, I would often see him in action for the last fifteen minutes of his show. It was plain to see, he was something of a misunderstood comic genius. It was Rob's slot that I was going to fill.

I had produced hundreds of shows and I had been interviewed many times, but being in charge, instigating the conversations was completely different. Each night I would try to work out what I was going to say in between the records and hope to make it through to the end of the show. It was very hard work but it seemed to go quite well. With the two-week period over, I went back into the studio to carry on working on the People's Praise project.

Out of the blue, I was approached to work on an album by

Aled Jones. I had sung with Aled a number of years earlier, but never actually met him. Chris Stuart was very friendly with Aled and his family and had written a song called 'Tell Me Boy' where an old man questions his younger self about how he has changed. I was the older version of Aled! That version was never released, although later in his career, Aled would replace me as the older voice. In 1987 he had just recorded a new album and I was asked to add extra instrumentation to the piano and vocal tracks. It was great to be a part of Aled's story although, as his voice was just about to break, the album wasn't heavily promoted. It would be a number of years before I would renew my acquaintance and friendship with Aled and have a small hand in helping him back into the charts.

It had been a strange year, full of unfulfilled promise and also life changing experiences. Both of the Hollies singles had failed to make the charts and, after thinking that Cliff Richard was going to record two of my songs, only one eventually saw the light of day turning up as a B side on the 12-inch version of his hit 'Some People'. In the real world I was now the father of two, Amy Rose and Jackson. There seemed to be enough work to keep us alive but 1988 was going to offer new challenges and opportunities.

CHAPTER 31

Good morning, Wales!

EVEN THOUGH 1987 HAD been good, the disappointments left quite a mark. To paraphrase John Cleese in the film *Clockwork*, the disappointment I could cope with, it was the hope that killed me. I found the constant waiting for people to make up their minds about my songs so soul-destroying that from that moment on I decided I wouldn't play the game – I wouldn't send songs to anyone who didn't ask for them. It was a strange decision, which meant that no one would record one of my songs for some time, but it gave me some sort of peace.

The gospel albums were coming thick and fast and, because Pete and I had set up a business to record the albums in our studio, it all sort of made sense. We were a little way into 1988 when I got a call from Megan Stuart née Emery. She had now married Chris Stuart and also become editor of BBC Radio Wales. She was planning some schedule changes and wanted to know if I would be interested in taking over the early morning show on a regular basis. Rob Brydon was going to move to London and there was an opportunity to take his place. I asked for a little time to think about it, but in my mind I knew it was too good an opportunity to turn down.

The new commitment was going to mean a lot of changes in lifestyle. With two young children I was used to waking up in the middle of the night, but this meant waking at 4 am every morning, driving to Cardiff for an hour's show that started at 6.25 am and then driving home to go back to bed for an hour before going back into the studio. It was hard, but for the first time in my life I had a regular source of income. Also, the daily radio presence seemed to create a new profile for me which led to more offers for other types of work.

On the day I started on the early show for BBC Radio Wales, in another studio close-by, Chris Stuart started presenting the early show for BBC Radio 2. After being the main voice of Radio Wales for almost ten years, Chris had been offered the early show on Radio 2 and the offer was too good to turn down. Eventually, he would have to relocate to London, but for the first few months he was allowed to do the show from Cardiff and we would often meet after our shows to share a BBC cooked breakfast. Chris had always been very supportive and he was one of the first I turned to when I was offered the show. I asked his advice and he told me that for the first month I should write every link from the first good morning to the final goodbye. He then said that after that month I wouldn't need to, it would just come naturally. To be honest, I didn't believe him as in the first few weeks I seemed to rely on my script implicitly but, almost to the day, I found the cards became unnecessary and I walked into the studio script-free.

The following year was a bit of a blur with early mornings turning into long studio days working on yet another gospel album. At least the daily commitment meant that I couldn't take on any tours or studio projects away from home. One of my big disappointments was being in Eastbourne when Amy had taken her first steps. I was desperate to make sure I didn't miss too many of the other big events in the lives of my two children, Amy and Jack.

In my mind, being a broadcaster is a bit like being a boxer or footballer. You can practise and train as much as you like, but you only learn how to do the job when you perform in front of a crowd. The early morning show was the perfect way to learn my trade, make my mistakes without the potential of falling flat on my face in front of too many people. As I clocked up more shows, I seemed to be getting better and my confidence was further boosted when I would occasionally be invited to sit in for other presenters on Radio Wales. Another thing I noticed was that as my broadcasting profile grew, offers started to come in from unexpected sources. I was starting to be invited to be a guest on TV shows for HTV Wales, becoming something of a regular musical guest on the *Elinor* chat show series and also making a guest appearance on an Owen Money special. For Owen's show, I performed one of my own songs and then joined Owen for a version of 'Great Balls of Fire'. Having been brought up on watching Elton John in concert, I decided towards the end of the song to kick away the piano stool and play to the end standing. The director Ronw Protheroe loved the move and showed the move in slow motion in the final edit.

It was late in November that I got a call from Ronw saying he'd been contacted by the Welsh Parliamentary Labour Party and had been asked to put together some sort of concert party to entertain the MPs at their Christmas party. Also joining the party was the tenor Mark Burrows. I was intrigued and, not knowing what to expect, I turned up at the HTV studios in my best suit carrying my guitar. We then drove to London where we were met at Black Rod's entrance and escorted via the back alleyways to the main courtyard beneath Big Ben. It was a crisp early December evening and the sound of the chimes from Big Ben seemed to echo through the Great Hall, a room which had remained largely unchanged for 1,000 years and where it was said, it was still possible to find tennis balls lodged in the oak beams, which had been sent there by the odd wayward shot from Henry VIII. It was hard not to be impressed as we passed the massive Christmas tree and climbed the stairs to enter the Jubilee rooms. These rooms served a number of purposes, but on this night, it was home to the Welsh Labour MPs. The long wooden tables were full of sandwiches and sausage rolls and at the back of the room a make shift bar had been set up with barrels of beer, perched precariously on the green leather committee chairs.

We didn't really know what was expected of us. I was worried because we had no amplification, but the room soon came to order on the arrival of the Official Leader of the Opposition, Neil Kinnock MP. It was the first time I had met Neil and I suppose, like so many other, I had allowed myself to be swayed by his portrayal in the media, especially by *Spitting Image*, but it was easy to see how he had come to lead the Labour Party at such a great time of change for the whole Labour movement. In his student days, he had teamed up with his future wife Glenys and it's said that people referred to them as 'the Power and the Glory', with Neil being the Glory. And, at first hand, you could see the glory, his charisma coming to the fore. The room was full of small groups eating and drinking and then he entered the room, surrounded by his entourage. With that entrance, the whole focus of the room it seemed, moved to centre about him. When he spoke, the room grew quiet. When he laughed, they all laughed. The power he wielded was almost tangible.

Straight away Neil became MC for the night. Holding his pipe in one hand, a pint in the other, he called for order as Mark and then I performed a couple of songs together. Then it was a time for everyone to perform their party piece. This was obviously normal as many MPs were asked by name to perform specific pieces. Neil himself joined in with a duet of 'The Beau Gendarmes' with the MP from Neath. Encouraged by the reaction, more MPs came forward and I was pressed into service with my guitar to provide the backing. The night took on a surreal quality as faces I had seen on television's *Question Time* or the *Six O'clock News* sang pop songs. Dr Jack Cunningham sang 'Blaydon Races', a Scottish MP, who someone said was a bit of a gangster, sang 'I Belong to Glasgow'. At one point one MP called for Neil to give a solo, only for him to be told by Neil "No, and there's no prizes for guessing who's going to be my new minister for Northern Ireland." At one stage Neil sang lead vocals, to be joined by a backing vocal section of Rhodri Morgan, Ron Davies and Allan Rogers.

At the end of the evening the MPs left for their various flats around the capital but we, as the concert party, were asked if we'd like to stay for a guided tour. We were taken through the beautifully deserted Great Hall where Kings, Queens and Prime Ministers from Gladstone to Churchill had lain in State. The lights from the giant Christmas tree provided a strange glow to the room and, as we passed by the steps where Charles I was condemned to death and the place where William Wallace had been tortured, the sense of history was overwhelming.

We were shown the green leathered main chamber of the House of Commons and then shown through to the official office of the Leader of the Opposition, where Neil Kinnock was waiting for us with a takeaway curry. Neil explained exactly how privileged we were. These were his private rooms. Many MPs had never been in there because they were only allowed into the room by special invitation. As we ate our curry, drank our House of Commons whisky and heard the Big Ben bells chime away the hours, I had to pinch myself to believe it was all happening.

The mood was broken by the sound of a woman's voice calling down the hallway. "Hurry up Neil; I've got school in the morning!" It was Glenys Kinnock. These were the days before she had become a full-time politician and her teaching job called for some sleep at least. After a final round of handshakes and hugs, Neil was gone and we were led back to our waiting cars. We hardly spoke on the way home, almost afraid to break some sort of magic spell. I'm proud to say that, with very few exceptions, I have made that annual Christmas pilgrimage to Westminster every since. In fact I've been performing at that annual event longer than many of the MPs have been MPs. The repertoire has changed somewhat over the years, marked most notably in my mind when one year we backed Kevin Brennan MP's version of 'Ziggy Stardust'. I have been fortunate to play for and sing for Chancellors, Prime Ministers, Lords, Ladies and MPs at this annual event. It has been a highlight and a source of memories that I will never take for granted and which I will never forget.

CHAPTER 32

Did I mention Rolf Harris and Catherine Zeta-Jones?

THE COMMITMENT OF EARLY morning daily radio meant that we had a family routine. I was still able to take the odd holiday to travel a little bit which meant I was still keeping my musical contacts intact. The luxury of a regular income meant I could pick and choose, so when Les Moir would offer a gig in Montreux playing piano for TV presenter and singer Sheila Wales, I could fly in and out and just have a good time.

What I was to learn was that broadcasting never stays the same for long. I had enjoyed the early show. I had learnt how to present and I was also able to juggle my musical commitments around my odd sleeping patterns. By this stage the show had also been moved to the BBC studios in Swansea. This made my life a lot easier as I didn't have an hour's drive to Cardiff every morning. Everything seemed in balance until Megan Stuart called me in for a meeting to say they were going to make changes to the schedule in the New Year and they would like me to present a new hour-long afternoon show. I think she was expecting a more enthusiastic response than I could give her. I realised that this was an incredible vote of confidence in me as a broadcaster, but saying yes would have a big impact on our lives. Over time, broadcasters come and go and the radio station carries on. Broadcasting can sometimes seem like a game of musical chairs, but when the music stops and you don't have a chair to sit on, life can get very difficult. I was broadcasting daily but also doing pretty well producing gospel albums. An afternoon programme would mean travelling daily to Cardiff and I would have to stop the music work. I asked for some time to think it over.

In many ways I had to say yes, the programme was too good an opportunity to turn down, but I did it with some nagging doubts in the back of my mind. The new programme would run from 4 pm until 5 pm and a new production team was put together including a young Oxford graduate called Paul Quinn. Paul brought in regular contributors like Paul Morley to review the week's television and he also suggested something which at the time I thought would never work. Paul knew of my musical background and suggested that we always keep a guitar handy so that if we got a musical guest in, I could pick up the guitar and jam with them. I was pretty sceptical at first, but the first guest we tried it with was Dennis Locorriere, the former lead singer of Dr Hook. He was told my musical background and was more than happy for us to do an unplugged version of 'Sylvia's Mother'. We came off-air and we were all elated. From then on, whenever the chance came for me to perform with a guest, we would.

One particularly memorable show was when Rolf Harris was the guest. Artists go in and out of fashion and this was just before his renaissance period. I had always been a Rolf fan and knew all the words to 'Two Little Boys'. The great thing about Rolf was his confidence and enthusiasm. He had no fear when it came to broadcasting and making music. His early recordings had been produced by Beatles producer George Martin, so no wonder they still sounded good. He showed me how to play the didgeridoo before joining me at the piano for 'Sun Arise'. Rolf was a great character and over the coming years would quite often phone me at home to let me know if he had a new album release or was coming to Wales.

Another guest was a young lady from Mumbles who had come to national recognition by starring in the Sunday evening TV show called *The Darling Buds of May*. I'd known about Catherine Zeta-Jones for some time as she had already been quite successful performing on the West End stage together with another Swansea girl, Ria Jones. The TV show turned her into a tabloid celebrity, so there was incredible excitement in the office when she arrived. Although I'd never met her before, we had a lot of Swansea friends in common and she seemed remarkably unspoilt by the media circus that surrounded her. Because I knew of her musical background, I managed to persuade her to join me for a song at the piano and one thing was sure, she really could sing.

It was a year or so later that I next saw her in the foyer of the BBC in Cardiff. She was sat in the corner wearing dark glasses trying to stay out of the limelight. I walked past and thought to myself, if it was anybody else from Mumbles in the foyer I would have said hello – why let her celebrity be a barrier to being friendly. I turned around and walked up to her. I thought I'd better re-introduce myself, in case she had forgotten me, but before I could finish off my sentence, "Hi Catherine, it's Mal Pope here from Mumbles..." she jumped up and gave me a big kiss. We talked for a couple of minutes and then I waved goodbye. Now the media is always a hotbed of gossip and I was worried that some people might have misinterpreted our greeting. The first thing I did when I got into the office was ring as many people as I could. Each conversation followed a similar pattern. "Hi, it's Mal Pope here. You might hear some gossip going around saying that I was spotted snogging Catherine Zeta-Jones in the foyer of the BBC. I have to tell you now that it's absolutely true!"

Broadcasting was now my occupation and I was growing in confidence. Although the BBC was my main employer I was getting regular approaches from HTV Wales for more music based shows. I had become quite friendly with a director called Emyr Afan. Emyr was definitely a young man in a hurry and, as we shared a similar church background, we had a lot in common. Emyr kept booking me for different shows, some in English and some in Welsh where I would struggle to recall the Welsh of my childhood as I performed.

In 1989 Emyr approached me with an offer of a one-off Easter music special. We had an hour to fill and we could do whatever we liked. I remember being on holiday in a caravan in Broad Haven, west Wales when I had an idea. I didn't really want to do the song, guest, interview sort of show. What if we tried to theme the songs and link them together in my best Dylan Thomas narrator's voice. Emyr seemed to like the idea and we spent a lot of time choosing the right songs to link together. This also gave me the opportunity to put right a wrong decision I had made many years previously. I had kept in touch with Tony Kiley and Wal Coughlan over the previous years and we had always said that at some stage we must get together. This was the perfect vehicle. Tony and Wal travelled down together from London and, for a couple of days over a weekend, we were the same kids who had rehearsed in my dad's garage all those years previously.

We filmed some of the tracks in the studio and the others on location. Filming coincided with Amy's fifth birthday and, as one of the songs on the show was called 'Amy' and was written for her, Emyr filmed the party which was hosted by Kev Johns or, as he was in those days, Clown Kev. The show was aired at Easter 1990 and got good viewing figures. It also left me enough tracks for my own album. With the financial security I had from TV and radio, I decided to set up my own record company. I had a lot to organise and at first, I was going to release a vinyl album. By the time everything had been completed it was obvious that vinyl was on its way out so *Love Will Find a Way* was MPH Records first release and it was a CD.

HTV seemed to be pleased with the show and over the next year or so I continued to work with Emyr on various projects. This was an interesting time for broadcasting in the independent sector because, with new licenses being granted for the various regions, everyone had to apply for a license under a secret bidding process. The competition for the HTV region appeared to be quite intense, with a number of interested parties making the running. I was approached by the HTV team. They were putting together their proposals for the new license and they wanted to add my name to the bid with my own musical chat show. Would I mind? I was delighted. The day came for the bids to be delivered and we all held our breath. The secret bids seemed to be fair but on reflection they were a disaster. The big regions had the opportunity to make the most money from advertising. They already had strong and wealthy companies incumbent. This strength made competitors wary and there didn't seem to be real competition for some of the franchises. Regions like HTV had less chance of making big advertising revenues but the competition was stronger as others felt they had a chance of taking control. There was a story that the man charged with putting in the bid for the Central license went to the office with two envelopes; one with a cheque for millions, the other with a cheque for a couple of thousand. He is said to have waited until the last moment and when he saw no rival bids being delivered, he put in the envelope with the smaller cheque. As a result Central Television won their bid unopposed ending up paying a fee to the government of £2,000 whereas HTV won their franchise with a cheque for £20.5 million.

I knew my name was attached to the bid, so I celebrated a little bit. But knowing how these things worked, I thought it wise not to get too excited. It did take some time for the dust to settle but true to their word, an autumn chat show was planned for 1993 and they still wanted me to be the presenter.

Chapter 33

The Mal Pope Show

By the early 1990s I was the proud father of three children – Lewis joining us late in 1989. The house in Morriston was just about starting to burst at the seams and it was obvious that we needed a bit more space. It took some time to find the right place, but with Hilary pregnant for the fourth time, we knew we had to take the plunge. With daily radio and the promise of a TV series, I borrowed more money than was sensible and moved the family to Mumbles. I knew it was the right house for us because, when I walked into the main bedroom, I opened the window and saw the Mumbles Lighthouse.

Daisy joined us on the 9th of April 1992. It was a day of mixed emotions. My Christmas trips to the House of Commons had continued and I had become quite a fan of Neil Kinnock. As the life span of the Parliament came to an end, he played less of a part in the annual party and it was interesting to see him become more serious and sharper over the years. The previous Christmas he had shown me a chair in the office of the official Leader of the Opposition. The chair had been sat on by them all: Churchill, Wilson, Thatcher. He had sat in that chair too long. "When I become Prime Minister, this chair is coming with me. And you're coming too. We'll have nights like this in Downing Street and Chequers." Daisy was born in the early hours of the Thursday morning and we were delighted to finally complete our family. I returned from visiting the hospital that evening to see the early results coming in from around the country. It wasn't long before I turned off the television and went to bed exhausted. It was pretty obvious from the exit polls that Neil Kinnock's and my Downing Street dreams were over.

Although HTV and BBC Wales might have been seen to be competitors, there didn't appear to be any problems with me working for both of them. Emyr and I started chatting regularly about the type of show we wanted to create and we seemed to be pretty much in agreement. Instead of a normal chat show, this would be a real musical chat show where guests would either be musicians who would be expected to illustrate what they were saying by playing live or well-known faces who loved music, who would be encouraged to talk about how much music meant to them.

The first sticking point for me was the sound. Over the years I had performed in numerous TV studios and the first thing that struck me was how bad the sound was that musicians had to work with. It was as if that was the last thing anyone thought about. I dug my heels in; if we were asking good musicians to put their reputations on the line by coming down to Wales to perform live, we had to be able to guarantee them concert quality sound. Emyr understood where I was coming from, but found it had to convince the accountants that we needed to spend money on equipment that no one would actually see on the screen. Eventually, that battle was won and it was on to the next one.

As well as sounding different, I wanted the show to look unlike any other TV show. On my afternoon radio show, I had met an unusual artistic collective named Klanger and Boink. They were photographers by trade but called themselves cultural engineers. They always wore sunglasses and identical white boiler suits with their names written on the back. It was quite a gimmick, but the thing that struck me was the quality of their work. It was fresh and inventive and like nothing I'd seen. I rang Emyr and told him that I had found the set designers. He wanted to know what TV sets they had designed before and I said they hadn't built any, but they were brilliant. We all met at HTV in Cardiff and true to form, they turned up in the suits. Everyone in the Light Entertainment department looked shocked. We had asked them to bring in some ideas which they presented to the production team. They had a set inspired by impressionist painters, with a giant Venus de Milo, clouds hanging from the ceiling and cactuses everywhere. Fair play to Emyr, many people would have wanted to play safe, but he bought into the whole idea and commissioned them to create our set.

The last thing I wanted was to have a London-based office for the show. I love Wales and know what we have here, but I also know there is a resistance to the unfamiliar and as far as London-based record companies were concerned, Wales in the early Nineties was almost unknown. I wanted us to work with Stuart Ongley, the man who published Cliff Richard and to use his contacts and his base at 101 Wardour Street, the old Rocket Records offices as our London base. Again, this had to be pushed through against the accountant's wishes, but at last we had a team I thought could make a great show.

The way we sold the show to the artists was that they would have the opportunity to play their current record and then they would be expected to join the house band to perform a cover. The house band would include Tony and Wal on bass and drums. The fact that they had played so many sessions in London encouraged the wavering guests to say yes. On keyboards was Chris Winter whose impressive CV and address book helped again and finally joining on guitar was Tim Hamill from Llanelli.

CHAPTER 34

It's Friday night and we're live...

THE SHOW WAS GOING to be broadcast live on a Friday evening. As it was so expensive to get the studio set up, we would also pre-record another show on the Thursday so that we had every other week off. We were all trying our best to bring in the biggest names we could using every contact we had. The problem was always going to be getting the first couple of names to say yes. We knew once we had some seal of approval, others would follow.

Although the show was going to be performed in front of a live audience, Emyr also wanted us to record some inserts for the show that would give us some breathing space in between live items. That summer, he'd also had a commission for a Welsh-language show which meant he had to be in New York. If we could scrape the money together for my flight, I could share a room with him and we could pick up a couple of interviews which would give us the glamour of the Big Apple.

Before we could start on my interviews, we had to record an insert for an S4C show based on the life of harpist Osian Ellis. We were going with Osian to view a harp that he had sold to a man named Leonard Stern on a previous trip to the States. Mr Stern lived on Fifth Avenue, in a house that had previously been the French Embassy. We were greeted by an armed guard and taken upstairs to meet the master of the house. It was obvious from the Van Goghs hanging on the walls that Mr Stern was wealthy; we had heard he owned a company that made pet food, but it turned out that he was billionaire who had liked the look of Osian's harp and had bought it as a piece of furniture for his house. He was very gracious and showed us all the works of art he had to hand. Then, he left us to carrying on filming. Emyr manoeuvred the harp into the centre of the room for Osian to play a piece for the camera. There was a model horse behind Osian which didn't look quite right, so Emyr picked it up and rather casually turned it to face the opposite direction. As part of our trip we had a couple of million pounds-worth of public liability insurance. When I pointed out to Emyr that he had just moved a Tang Dynasty horse and if he'd dropped it our insurance wouldn't have covered it, he did lose a little bit of colour from his face.

We had a couple of interviews lined up for the show. Downtown Julie Brown was a real New York celebrity, having come to prominence in the States as one of the early DJs on MTV. To me, she was Julie Brown from Bridgend, who had been crowned World Disco Dancing Champion in 1979 and I'd met her through Megan Stuart at Radio Wales who had tried to get her into broadcasting in Wales. We recorded the interview in the back of a black stretch limo and she showed me the sights of the city by opening the sun roof. As we drove through the New York streets, people kept calling out her name.

The next interview was with a harpist Deborah Henson-Conant whom Emyr had worked with at a Welsh harp festival. She wasn't your typical harpist, preferring to play standing up and dressed in leather and stilettos. Emyr had arranged for us to play together at the top of a skyscraper, the building where *Home Alone* star Macaulay Culkin lived. As always, the roof wasn't good enough for Emyr and he had us climb over the wall to a balcony, so that he could get the perfect shot of the New York skyline.

The big coup for our trip was an interview with John Cale from the Velvet Underground. Emyr had booked the

Rainbow Rooms at the top of the Rockefeller Centre. We were all set up and waiting as we'd been told he could be a bit prickly. He looked healthy although his skin was slightly orange, which he attributed to his latest fad of drinking copious amount of carrot juice. He was funny, lively and entertaining. Having got quite a long interview, I thought I'd got to know him well enough to test our new friendship. I asked him when it came to the early days of the Velvet Underground was it not so much avant-garde as haven't practised. He stopped for a moment, smiled and answered the question with all the good humour and contempt it deserved. With a stock of good interviews in the can, we headed home.

The idea for the show was that we were performing in a club somewhere in Wales. A few weeks prior to the first show, we filmed the opening sequence at a disused theatre in Barry. We had the street closed off and big search lights beaming out into the night sky as various friends of Klanger and Boink danced in the backlit windows. The idea was that I would walk into the building wearing a big black overcoat and we would cut into the studio where I would walk onto the set, take off my coat, hang it on a big yellow coat hanger before taking to the stage to join my band for the first song of the evening.

With John Cale on our guest list we found other artists easier to book. Our first show was recorded in front of a live audience on a Thursday night. The headline act was George Melly and I got to sing 'Won't You Come Home Bill Bailey' with George and his band. We also had an interview and performance from the percussionist Evelyn Glennie together with the John Cale interview in New York. There was a real sense of excitement in the studio that night but nothing compared with the following night. This would be our first show in the series and would be absolutely live. Guests included Go West, jazz saxophonist Andy Shepherd, singer-songwriter Martyn Joseph and a pre-recorded interview with Beverley Craven.

We rehearsed throughout the day and even performed a 30-second live trail up to the *Ten O'clock News*, with me talking as the band played. By the time the news had ended, the feeling in the studio was literally electric. The floor manager counted down the seconds and then cued Tony on the drums. He counted the band in and the title we recorded in Barry played out. On cue, I walked into shot, took off my coat, walked onto the stage as the band kicked into 'Keep On Running'. Wal had a couple of brass playing friends down for the weekend, so they joined us too. It was that sort of show. The hour flew by in what felt like minutes. I had decided I didn't want autocue and just about managed to get through the links without too much trouble. After the show in the Green Room, we all turned and hugged each other; it had been a great couple of days.

The show was full of highlights for me. One was an interview with Cliff Richard. Cliff had recorded some of my songs, so we weren't complete strangers but the organisation that surrounded him was very protective. We met at a studio in Shepperton where he was rehearsing for a tour. I had brought my guitar with me, but kept it at a safe distance. We finally got a camera set up and were all set to start the interview. I turned to Cliff and said, "Would you mind if we did the interview with our guitars." He looked at me for what seemed like hours but was, in reality, only seconds. "What do you mean?" he asked. I took a deep breath and said, 'Well if we're talking about a song like 'Summer Holiday', maybe you could show me how it goes and we could play a bit of it together." I realised that there was every chance we could be thrown off-set as this hadn't been agreed to and cleared by the management. Again, after what seemed like an age he agreed and reached for a guitar and we were off. In fact, we had to reload the camera because we ran out of tape. At heart Cliff is someone who loves music and when asked to talk about his favourite subject, he can't be stopped.

Other highlights included Suzanne Vega and Mica Paris but my favourite show was the Christmas Special. We had managed to get Dave Edmunds on the show by paying for a return flight from his home in LA. Bonnie Tyler didn't have that far to come, but she stormed the show with a great version of 'It's A Heartache'. Howard Jones, who in reality is also a Swansea boy, joined us for a solo performance to kick the show off with a bang, and joining us late (as he had a meeting in London he couldn't miss) Neil Kinnock popped in for a bit of a Christmas chat. The finale was a dream. We had managed to arrange for two old friends of Dave Edmunds to join us, the guitarist Mickey Gee and from Dire Straits, the drummer Terry Williams. They played the opening two numbers but to bring the show to an end, we settled on 'Run Rudolph Run' and everyone joined in. Bonnie shared vocals and Howard Jones played Hammond organ. We had Terry and Tony both playing drums together and, as the snow began to fall, the audience left their seats and joined in the party. The credits rolled and that should have been it, but no one wanted to go home. I looked at Dave and said, "Shall we?" "Why not?" he replied. With that he counted in 'I Hear You Knocking'. And the band played on as the crew left their cameras and the production staff left the gallery to join in the fun. As we left the studio, I remember thinking to myself, how can we ever top that?

CHAPTER 35

Everything's going so well, what could possibly go wrong?

THE SHOW SEEMED TO be well-received all round. I got a lovely letter from the Head of HTV Wales and the show went on to win a couple of Welsh BAFTA Awards. The following spring a series of interviews recorded for the show were shown, including longer versions of the interviews with John Cale and Beverley Craven and a Special which we had recorded with Dave Edmunds whilst he was over at Christmas. Plans were underway for a new series in the autumn of 1994 and life was good. The kids were enjoying school and we were really starting to fit into village life in Mumbles, making lots of new friends.

The radio show had moved back to Swansea which meant I didn't have the daily drive to Cardiff, but it also meant I wasn't a regular face in the office either. The figures were good for the show, so I wasn't particularly worried. That summer we heard the news that the next series was in a bit of trouble. HTV where starting to think of ways that they could meet their financial commitment to the government; cutbacks were the order of the day. The next series would be one show less than the first. At one stage it looked as if Channel 4 might take the show to their network, but in the end they went for a relatively normal pop show based in London.

I decided I needed to make another record. I had made a 5-track EP prior to the first TV series, thinking that the national press might help encourage guests. It got featured on Steve Wright's afternoon show and picked up some late Radio 1 plays; the ripples of interest it created helped with my profile. The following spring I recorded another 5-track EP and released 'Golden Days' as a single. Bob Harris immediately picked up on the track and played it almost every night on his radio 1 radio show. It was also getting a good reaction from the playlist producers and was even listed to be played on the top-rated Simon Bates programme. I listened to the show from start to finish and was later rung by my radio plugger to be told that we'd been bumped because an interview about a guy lying in a bath of beans over ran.

The second series went to another technical level as we all knew exactly what we should be doing. The guest list was again impressive including the Bee Gees, Paul Young and Justin Haywood from the Moody Blues. The Christmas Special featured a terrific performance of 'Total Eclipse Of The Heart' from Bonnie Tyler with more dancing and more snow, but this time at the end of the series, there was no letter of congratulations. In fact, there was nothing at all. Emyr tried his best to find out what was happening but after some time, it became clear that the show wouldn't be re-commissioned. They were going to find a cheaper alternative.

At least I had my radio show to rely on. I still remember the meeting in a little office in Swansea. They always say you never hear the bullet which has your name on it and this bullet came silently out of nowhere. Paul Evans was my producer and over the year or so working together in Swansea every day we had become pretty good friends. He looked shocked and very serious. "There's no easy way to say it Mal, I've just had a call from Cardiff. They want to make some schedule changes and they are taking the afternoon show off the air. They are going to give you something instead but it won't be every day." I went cold and my head went into overdrive. I have rarely felt so many emotions all at the same time: numb, angry, disappointed, shocked, embarrassed and most of all, sick to the pit of my stomach. I had four children, a big mortgage and in a month's time I would be unemployed. My first thought was how could God let this happen; my second was how do I tell Hilary; my third thought – how on earth do I get out of this?